FULL SPECTRUM CYBERWAR

A Novel by

Ed Mahoney

Full Spectrum Cyberwar
KDP ISBN 978-1-0914-8355-2
Paperback 1st Edition, March 2019

Copyright © 2019 by Ed Mahoney

Cover Art is licensed for this novel from:
Cyber War - Stock Image | Portugal2004 | Stock photo ID: 172709336
https://www.istockphoto.com/photo/cyber-war-gm172709336-5356215

Published by Lobo Media Ltd.
Lobo Media Ltd.
1805 S. Coffman St., Longmont CO 80504
http://lobomedia.press

Follow the author at HTTP://arunnersstory.com
Other books by the author: Cyber War I

Hardcover: 978-1-7923-0681-5
Paperback: 978-1-0914-8355-2
E-Book: 978-1-7923-0680-8

PRINTED IN THE UNITED STATES OF AMERICA

This story wasn't all mine. I shared it with friends.

Robert Graham of Durango was the first to read my manuscript and provide his unique critique. I'll even give him credit for his monthly coaching exercises, joined by his collection of writing proselytes.

David Dubois, a cybersecurity product manager, followed with his commentary on the credibility of my technical conjecture. I took a few more liberties with tech before David read this.

Sometimes with coffee, other times with wine, I especially enjoyed my feedback sessions with Leigh Ann Dillinger, from across the street.

And then, I have to believe that if my friend Wendy Spurbeck wasn't such a strong force in the astronautics industry, she would be highly successful as an editor. This story is so much better, thanks to these good friends.

To all you techies who RTFM along with the EULA.

Chapter One

THE day was indisciplined, with drinking through breakfast, lunch, and dinner. Retirement wasn't far away.

To be well prepared for Mondays, Rob rarely drank on Sundays, but the morning began by eating brunch at Lucile's with his wife, drinking two Bloody Marys each. After a short nap, Sue and he found themselves splitting a lunch plate at a restaurant perched high on a hillside overlooking town. Still sitting there at four in the afternoon, outdoors on the terrace, he ordered a second bottle of wine. They were enjoying themselves, knowing they were weeks away from retiring, years earlier than expected, massively wealthy with the sale of Rob's software firm.

"It's not that I can't handle the winters, Rob. The problem with living in a mountain town is we might not have ready access to healthcare at a time in our lives when we're going to start needing it."

"I'm talking about ski resorts. Vail has a very nice hospital, just blocks away from Lionshead."

"This is the first time you've mentioned Vail. You've been talking Telluride. The best healthcare there is probably their vet clinic for livestock."

"Oh, I'm sure they have something. I know lots of people retire in Ridgway. That's only twenty miles away."

"You're not going to want to drive twenty miles for every little doctor's appointment. Not in the winter."

"We can queue up visits in the summer. And drives will be

1

gorgeous with the aspens turning in the fall."

Sue relented. She was proud of her husband and wanted him to fulfill his dreams in retirement. "You think you'll be hiking mountain trails the rest of your days, don't you?"

"That's the plan."

"Well, that's fine with me. You deserve it. But we need to do some further research on the right town. I'm going to look into Aspen. Does Aspen have good trails?"

"They're okay." Rob downplayed Aspen, but he knew they'd be able to afford it and he wouldn't mind living there. "I just know that our grandchildren would love to visit us if we lived near a ski resort. It'll be fun taking them hiking and backpacking in the summers."

"You're already planning on grandchildren. Oh my." Sue made a surprised face, even though she was the one who usually broached the topic with their two kids. "I'll miss living in Boulder. We raised our kids here. I can see our house from here."

"No way."

"Sure. Look, do you see the hospital over there?"

"I see commercial buildings. I can't make out which is the hospital."

"Are you losing your eyesight before me? Look. Surely you can make out Broadway. Follow it north until it reaches the hospital. Then look east. Right there."

"All I see are trees."

"Maybe you should check the prescription on those hipster bifocals of yours. I really do think you might be aging quicker than me, honey."

"It's not the years, honey, it's the miles."

"Oh, you think you're Indiana Jones now." Sue laughed. "Your hair is half gray, mister."

"Yours probably is too. It's just hard to see because you're blonde."

"Hard for you to see, you mean."

Rob looked, and he couldn't see any gray in Sue's hair. She never admitted to coloring her hair, but he'd seen debit card receipts for over a hundred dollars. He found it specious that women's haircuts were over one hundred dollars. He was also seasoned enough in the role of husband to know that pushing this line of conversation could only get him into trouble, so he changed topics.

"My partners should be arriving in the next thirty minutes or so for dinner. You want to join us?"

"No, I'm tired. I have a full day tomorrow showing houses. Summer is when us realtors make our money."

"You won't be doing that for much longer, sweetie. Time to start winding down your client list."

"I think you're right. You enjoy your dinner, honey. I'm going to ping an Uber."

Sue ubered home, leaving Rob waiting for his business partners to join him to plan for the upcoming week. Two of them flew in from Austin earlier in the day to negotiate the sale of their firm to a large, local tech corporation.

***

Rob considered the Flagstaff House to be a destination restaurant, and explained it as such to his dinner guests early Sunday evening, still seated outside on the hill overlooking the city of Boulder, Colorado.

"This place was originally built as a summer cabin, before the Great Depression. It became this restaurant over sixty years ago."

Rob was joined for dinner by three of his five Response Software business partners. Bill Thompson was a long-time friend and colleague from his previous firm, CBI. Marco Lopez was only twenty-eight years old and it was his LLC, Response Software, they initially invested in to start their venture. And Dylan Moore was not much older at thirty-four, and the owner of another software firm called Automated Responder that they merged with Response Software a year earlier to form a larger outfit.

Marco, a partner who also lived in Boulder, challenged Rob. "But it's not really a destination restaurant. I mean, it's within the city limits. It only took me ten minutes to drive here."

Rob defended his position. "I don't think there's a mileage metric to define destination restaurants. We're sitting two thousand feet above the city. And that was a pretty damned steep drive."

Bill knew Rob well enough to know when he was making inane chit-chat rather than serious conversation. Marco, in addition to being quite young, was an extremely nerdy type who missed social clues and seemed to be thinking of this as a serious business-planning meeting, whereas Bill understood Rob to consider this a celebration.

He also knew Rob had been sitting on this terrace drinking wine with his wife since lunch, before the rest of them arrived for dinner. Rob and Sue had reason to celebrate. Like all of them, they were a few weeks away from becoming multi-millionaires.

Bill interjected to help Marco understand the nature of the dinner meeting. "Destination or not, this is a damn fine restaurant. Awesome place to celebrate our pending sale of Response Software to CBI. Cheers everyone."

They clinked their wine glasses and Dylan contributed to the discussion.

"Rob, I wish you could join us for the negotiations this week with CBI. You know them, having worked most of your career there."

Rob responded, "Probably best I don't attend. I'm sort of persona non grata after being fired last year."

"But Bill is okay? He worked there too?"

"They didn't fire Bill. He quit on his own. Besides, someone needs to lead this pen test in the U.K. next week. We need Greg down in Austin working on our next code drop."

Marco said, "I should be down there leading that effort."

"We need someone here with deep technical skills to baffle the lawyers," replied Bill.

Rob and Dylan both grunted and laughed in agreement. Dylan added, "Well Rob, I hate seeing you have to work so hard, having to travel overseas, when you should be planning your retirement. Sue must be excited. Retiring wealthy a good ten years before you planned?"

"She is. We had a good day sitting out here today, planning our future. I'm plenty willing to take one more bullet for the team. Don't you boys worry about me."

***

There are two types of hikers. The athletic thrill-seeker who explores challenging terrain, remote wilderness, dramatic exposure, and epic adventure. The other is satisfied with pedestrian strolls. Rob Warner preferred hikes in mountainous terrain, above tree line, full-day, three thousand calorie-burning treks. The Continental Divide Trail was a perfect example, and his go-to trail.

The Norfolk Coast Path along the North Sea in the U.K., with its flat sea marsh and plodding sand dunes, wouldn't seem on paper to entice a hiker like Rob. But it was remote in that it was out of the country. And it had cliffs. It wasn't as dramatic as the Scottish

Highlands, but it would offer one-of-a-kind scenery.

Sue was surprised to see Rob set his travel bag on the bed and start packing.

"You leaving me?"

"I'm going to hike the Norfolk Coast Path. Been on my wishlist for years. Finally got a business trip in the region."

"Where is this trail?"

"The U.K."

Sue found it incredulous that Rob was taking this trip. He could have told her during their long lunch date at the Flagstaff House. She usually put on one of the outfits Rob liked and gave him a sensual sendoff before he traveled internationally. *How could he not have figured that out by now? Does he really believe it's just a coincidence? Hiking must dull his brain.* She was already in bed, and at fifty-five, she liked a good eight hours, preferably twenty-four hours, to get in the mood.

"Rob, you're selling Response Software to CBI in a couple of weeks for over one hundred million dollars. We're going to Maui in four weeks. You should be packing for that, mister."

"One more business trip, sweetie. With Marco helping to negotiate the transaction in Boulder and Greg leading a code drop in Austin, I need to lead a pen test on a wind farm in the North Sea. Although honestly, it's mostly about the hike."

"So, to be clear, you're not still trying to grow the business?"

"Right, it's all about the hike. Can't pass this up."

Rob was fifty-five years old too, and ready to retire. Retirement was all he'd thought about for the last ten years, except when he was thinking about hiking. Living near the foothills of the Front Range in Colorado, he had ample opportunity for local hikes, but leveraging an international business trip to hike a storied trail was like hitting a hole-in-one for a golfer. He packed his clean pair of trail shoes to avoid getting dirt on his business shirts.

"I will say though, we rarely do penetration tests. K.C. is coming along to add to her automation use cases. It'll be interesting work."

"I can't believe you're still taking on more work."

"Well, we've been working with this customer for the last month, collecting data remotely. Our client backlog will add to our final sale price. I just decided today to join the travel team after checking the weather. Supposed to be perfect on Friday for a hike."

"Will you be earning Maui points at the hotel?"

"There's no Marriott in this town Sue, but I will on my flight." Rob wasn't clear as to why Sue still insisted on scoring travel points when they would soon be wealthy, but he figured it was easier to appease her than to argue that point.

"Just you and K.C.?" Sue wasn't truly jealous of K.C., she knew too much about her. Still, pregnant or not, the Chinese-American woman was very young and drop-dead gorgeous.

"Justin is coming too."

Sue was relieved to hear this. Justin was one of Rob's partners in the firm. *Safety in numbers.*

"I wish you'd have told me last week. I would have gone with you."

"Sorry, sweetie. Greg was going to lead this, but he's trying to complete that major code drop before the CBI transaction. He just asked me this afternoon if I could do it and, after checking the weather, I couldn't turn it down. The Norfolk Coast Path, Sue. In the peak of summer."

"Right. I get it. How long?"

"Unless I actually discover a major breach, or fall off a cliff hiking, I'll be back Saturday."

***

Justin expected the North Sea to be treacherous, like it appeared in movies, with twenty-five-foot waves, cold with clouds kissing the water, stormy gray with day indistinguishable from night. Instead, he was standing comfortably inside the raised pilothouse of a thirty-foot, 600 horsepower, fast trawler, at 9 am in the middle of the calmest water he'd ever seen for an ocean. He imagined himself waterskiing on this glass as he scanned for radio signals from a laptop app, designed especially for this purpose.

He already knew the wifi server name. The two-man crew who operated this crew transfer vessel, this CTV, told him, but he wanted to try out all the features of his hacking stack. He also wanted to continue his waterski daydream, visions crossed his mind nearly progressing it to an augmented reality movie, but he wasn't alone in his work.

Standing over his shoulder, monitoring every step of his progress, was Claire Mcintyre, the Chief Information Security Officer. She was CISO of Mistral Controls, the wind farm operations firm that hired Justin and his firm to *ethically* hack into their network.

Claire looked to Justin as he imagined all women C-levels to appear, dressed in a black pinstriped suit jacket and matching below-the-knee skirt and green blouse, not quite shoulder-length, ginger hair combed straight back behind her ears - like John Travolta in Pulp Fiction.

Thin and tall for a woman at five foot, nine inches, she wasn't unattractive at forty years of age. Justin wouldn't kick her out, but he could see how she might be high maintenance. She hadn't stopped questioning him the entire boat ride from Lowestoft, the tourist and fishing village where Claire's firm maintained the operations center to control this 504-megawatt wind farm located fourteen miles offshore from Suffolk, England.

Claire, embarrassed that the wifi servers on her wind turbines didn't require passwords, justified her rationale with each question to Justin.

"If we didn't tell you the wifi server name Justin, how would you find it? I ask because, as you'll soon see, the wifi servers don't broadcast their SSIDs. This isn't Starbucks."

"I don't need to know the Service Set Identifier, Miss Mcintyre. What you see running on my screen right now is an SSID scanner. And it just published for me the wifi server name. Mistral Wind Turbine 43."

"Hmm. Is that application something you downloaded from the Dark Web?"

"No. Wifi scanner apps like Kismet or Aircrack are the sort of thing you would find on the Dark Net, but you can google them just as easily. This is a commercial app that came with the wifi system we operate at my firm's home office. And now, as you can see, my laptop is on your wind farm's wifi network." Justin displayed the network connection info to Claire.

"Okay, I see." Claire was undeterred. "But you would still have to actually log onto something, and it's not like we host Microsoft Windows servers inside these towers. Our *air gap* security architecture I described to you and your team yesterday still applies. This network is not accessible from the Internet. It might appear buggered that we don't password-protect the wifi, but think about it.

"You have to be on a boat within range of these towers to access our wifi. We don't apply passwords because our maintenance technicians can't remember them and the cost of constantly educating them isn't worth the trouble. Security is always a risk equation, Justin. Cost of security versus operational convenience."

"I get that, but just to let you know, I'm already in. I now own this network."

"What? How did you do that so quickly?"

"While you were talking, I scanned for systems within this tower. There are only a few. Then I scanned for vulnerabilities. The Ethernet switch inside this tower is an industrial Antaira LNX-802NS3. The default IP address is 192.168.1.254 and default username and password are admin and admin. Hard to rationalize not changing the defaults on those. From here I can access every wind tower in this wind farm, since this switch connects all of them via a fiber ring, and they all contain identical ethernet switches, likely all still configured with their default settings."

Justin looked expectantly at Claire after this statement, hoping the vulnerability scan continuing to run returned more potential systems for him to exploit while she talked.

"Point taken Justin, but let me reiterate. When I say this network is air-gapped, there is absolutely no connectivity to the Internet. The boats can connect to the towers via wifi. And there is radio connectivity from our boats back to our operations center onshore for limited telemetry, but those systems are not connected to the Internet either. It's a closed network. There would be absolutely no way if these systems were breached, for the malware to ever call home to command and control servers."

"I understand, and I agree. However, constant communication with C2 servers isn't always necessary. It's useful to exfiltrate data or in botnets to update the malware for various purposes such as spam campaigns or denial of service attacks, but the first step in defeating an air gap security architecture is simply the initial breach itself. And we can now see how that's possible. By someone traveling out here on a boat within range of the wind farm's wifi.

"And let me just say that since you've been talking, I've now discovered that there is, in fact, a Microsoft Windows server on this network. The controller for this tower is a Windows 2003 Server, which is odd considering this wind farm was built between 2008 and 2012. That's considered by many to be the most vulnerable operating system in history. I've already exploited it and am in the middle of copying the server image onto my hard drive."

Justin did his best not to sound smug, but he felt good about himself just now.

"I see. Well, that's a clanger, isn't it? How long would it take you to hack into the other system components?"

"Assuming they're identical, a few minutes each. I'll capture as many server images as we have time for and research them back onshore. I might not have enough time to discover any intrusions in time for our presentation tomorrow, but I'll continue to analyze the images over the next couple of weeks and share with you my findings."

"Smashing plan."

Claire turned silent, drifting outside the pilothouse while reading her smartphone. Justin completed his work under the shadow of the immense wind farm blades, eerily still in the windless day, as the boat returned to Lowestoft.

***

Twenty miles offshore, watching the horizon of water remain just that, looking for signs of Lowestoft from the pilothouse on their return, Justin considered what he might find in the server images he captured from the wind farm. He only sampled five servers from five towers, because capturing images from the entire wind farm would have taken all day or longer, but he was able to download logs from all thirty-three systems. His team's presentation was due to Claire and her management team tomorrow afternoon, and he now had the information needed for that report.

He'll state that the open wifi, as implausible as it may seem in the middle of the North Sea, was wide open for attack, and he did hack his way in. Which was of course the objective of this ethical hack engagement.

It would have been nice to have four days for this assignment but his partner Rob Warner insisted they take three days and present their findings Thursday afternoon, so that they could squeeze in a hike along some shoreline cliffs Friday, before flying home Saturday. Justin was new to all this and wished he possessed Rob's confidence. He was like Rob in his own core proficiency of data networking, but computer security was a new career to him. With that as his last thought, Justin looked over at the boat captain and tried to strike up a conversation.

"Doesn't seem to be a lot of birds out here. The wind farm pretty good at whacking them out of the sky?"

Justin didn't mean anything by this other than it was the first thing that came to mind. He understood it was the wrong thing to say as soon as the boat captain turned his gaze back at him to respond.

"You one of shose American snowflakes, son? Worriedt about the birdts?"

The captain had a thick Dutch accent, although Justin didn't know it was Dutch, only that it was hard to understand.

"Snowflake?"

"Let me tell you someshing, son." The boat captain wasn't listening to Justin's responses any more than he was looking at him after that first scowling glance, his eyes alternating between the horizon and his instruments.

"Dese wind farms don't kill birds no more than nature herself. I can quote you da stats from your own continendt. Windt farms in America kill about a quarter million birdts a year. Soundt like a lot to you son?" He didn't wait for Justin to answer.

"Oil and gas pits kill over shree times dat. Still, dat's noshing. Your electrical lines in America kill over swenty-five million birdts a year. Cars kill swo hundredt million. Windows from buildings kill anosher shree hundred million. But all dat is noshing because cats kill over swo billion birdts a year. Cats! Now you shink about dat, son."

"Hmm." Justin generally avoided cultural activities when he traveled and this conversation was just another reason why. For something else to do, he'd like to begin scanning the server images for signs of being breached, but the application scanner he used for that was cloud-based and he'd have to wait to return to his hotel for connectivity.

Already deep in thought, Justin was startled when the boat captain started the dialog back up.

"I understandt you're a hacker son. I know a little aboudt hacking. My son works on computers. You a white hadt or a black hadt?"

Justin was impressed to hear those terms enough to believe this old man might actually know what a hacker was.

"Using those terms, I'm a white hat. I'm the good guy. We call it ethical hacking or pen testing, short for penetration testing."

This was his first time to perform an ethical hack and he found it interesting. He joined Response Software nearly a year ago after working with its partners, Rob, Bill, and Greg, on a cyber hack into their previous employer, a giant IT services outsourcing firm named Cyber Business International, or CBI. Rob and he were fired due to their respective roles in that cluster. Almost immediately, they formed this new firm to offer computer security incident response services. Ethical hacking wasn't part of their standard offerings, but Bill, their business development executive - BDE - wanted to establish a beachhead in the energy industry, and they had the skills.

"So the lady is paying you to hack her network to learn how to protect it?"

"That's exactly right."

Justin knew better than to share too much with this boat captain. He understood this energy firm was interested in understanding their security posture. He wasn't so sure Claire was onboard with that mission. She'd been overly defensive all morning. The fact she insisted on attending his attempt to hack into the wind farm demonstrated that at minimum, she was a control freak. Or maybe she wanted to be prepared to defend herself tomorrow.

"I heard you say to the lady that you were successful with your hacking. I didn'dt understandt all your technical wordts. Is shis company in trouble?"

"I can't say. It'll take me some time to review my server images."

If this assignment followed their typical service of responding to cyber attacks, he would spend this week performing forensics. He'd capture information, generally server images, and interview IT staff, then spend the next two or three weeks back home parsing through the data to determine the attack vector and the impact. How the attack occurred, what systems were breached, and what critical data were exfiltrated.

Ethical hacking was different. His team provided with sensitive system information two weeks earlier via email and conference calls, such as IP addresses and network diagrams, to spare the time of reconnaissance any hacker could ultimately perform. They were taking this week to compromise the perimeter systems from the Internet, or in today's case, from the North Sea, and present their findings to the client.

"I doubt it's anything to worry about, Captain."

***

Claire sat behind the pilothouse in the open stern of the trawler.

She imagined Justin and the crew were making lewd comments about her. She'd overheard the crew talking before. *Screw them, she has work to do.* She won't be online for the next hour, but she didn't need to be. She engaged herself by drafting multiple emails on her Samsung Galaxy 8 to her staff to prepare for tomorrow's meeting, to defend herself against what she expected these American data cowboys to present.

They might avoid outright pomposity in order to be invited back, but they'll be smug toward her. Everything they present, like this open wifi in the middle of the bloody sea, will be perceived as an attack against her and her staff, suggesting she failed in her mission to maintain prudent information security. *Consultants are such buggers. She'll weather this storm.*

Chapter Two

SARA Thomas was a serious-minded sixteen-year-old. With two years of high school behind her, her petite 5'1", 95-pound frame led people to guess she was only headed into 8th grade. She got her share of double takes during night classes for the college level calculus she attended Tuesday and Thursday nights at Austin Community College. Most boys considered her pretty, but she didn't know that. She wasn't so dorky as to wear over-sized glasses, her specs were hip wireframes, but she'd yet to start thinking about boys. Sara's focus was elsewhere.

This was her second month working at Response Software, in their modern office complex off Loop 360, overlooking Lake Austin. She got the job after meeting a Captain Calvert of the U.S. Cyber Command, the previous summer while attending a Black Hat conference in Las Vegas with her father. Captain Calvert, now a major, stayed in touch with her father, and Calvert's wife K.C., who worked for the cybersecurity forensics firm, offered Sara the job in May.

She expected today to be like all the others. Jen, her team lead and official mentor as the only other female on-site, tended to sit down with her around 10 am on Wednesday mornings to teach her a new software tool. Software that Jen referred to as being part of their forensics toolkit or stack, which implied a set of tools that all work together.

Sara was in her cube before 8 am, reading her email. She had one marked urgent from Justin Peters, whom she understood to be pretty high up in the firm, one of the partners. Sara had never received an email before with the urgent flag set. She read it first.

Sara,

Jen tells me you're up to speed on the ELK stack. That's awesome. I need you to query these 45 days worth of server logs six ways from Sunday and let me know if you find any interesting patterns. If you have time, <u>download this server image</u> too and compare it against the standard image we already have. I need your findings by EoD.

JP

Sara googled "six ways from Sunday." *Oh, he wants an exhaustive search. Fun.* Next, Sara googled "EoD." *My end of day or his?*

Sara detached the archived file from the email, saved it to her hard drive, then decompressed it to find a trove of over a thousand log files from thirty-three separate servers. She added these logs to the data lake she had been building as part of her internship. That data store was comprised of massive storage in the Amazon cloud offering termed AWS S3 for Amazon Web Services Simple Storage Service.

She began to study the files by scrolling through their file names. It was apparent there were thirty-three different servers, as their hostnames contained unique numbers, each with forty-five logs, and that each log captured data over a twenty-four hour period. Fourteen hundred and eighty-five server logs.

She opened up all the logs at once using her ELK stack to color code each unique data point over the entire forty-five days. Her program determined the normal range of readings based on statistical analysis, and illustrated meaningful deviations from the norm with the colors. Color patterns emerged across most of the data points, for each server, on each day, until the final hour. *Maybe that's normal and the final day's readings are anomalous because Justin didn't get a full day?*

Sara drilled down into the data points by clicking on them. The logs contained readings that she didn't understand. She did understand each row of data was timestamped every thirty seconds. And she caught visually, by the color-coded representation, that the readings were entirely identical across each of the thirty-three servers, until the final hour of the last day. Her guess was that the data points flagged by her pattern-matching software should probably be more random, like the final hour readings.

She googled wind farms and stumbled upon some information from the Department of Energy that explained the readings to her. "rev/s" referenced the rotation of the turbine in revolutions per second. "m/s" was a meters per second reading of the wind speed. There were other readings for power output and pitch. Every color-coded reading was identical, until the final hour, as if all thirty-three servers were running the same control program. Sara wasn't deep enough in her knowledge of this tech to know to what extent these systems were machine controlled, but clearly, windspeed came from nature and would have to be random.

She spent more of her time reading online details of how wind farms operated than reviewing the logs themselves. The ELK stack did all the log analysis for her within a few minutes. The real effort was in understanding the significance of her findings. She also had time to download the server image from a link included in Justin's email, and run the compare. Sara emailed her findings back to Justin before her 10 am meeting with Jen.

Chapter Three

THE weather in Norfolk took a turn early Thursday morning, with rain as hard as Rob had ever seen. It was 9 am and he couldn't say with any certainty that the sun ever rose. He was distracted by thoughts of having to cancel his hike tomorrow and found it difficult to stay on task as he huddled with his two team members, Justin and K.C., in his hotel room. Their breakfast trays and coffee were spread out on his twin-size mattress, while he stood and Justin and K.C. sat at two chairs around a small, round table.

They debated how to respond to Justin's findings. Not his discovery of open wifi on the high seas, but of the breach he discovered late at night while reading Sara's report on the server images.

"Okay, before we get too excited, can we please just finish this slide detailing the end-to-end data communications network?"

Rob understood K.C. was right that more discovery was required and they needed to share their results with a larger community, but he'd be the one presenting in five hours and wanted to finish his slides.

"Justin, let me walk through this one more time. Tell me if this is right.

"The operations control center is a single room in Lowestoft, staffed with one to three techs twenty-four, seven, completely isolated from the Internet.

"Their computers are never updated online, rather they have their images refreshed quarterly.

"Telemetry is a two-step process. The ops center maintains a data connection with radio signals to the CTVs, to download operating logs collected from the wind farms. Those boats first retrieved the logs from the wind farms via wifi when within range. So, wifi to RF. And as needed, they configure the control servers onboard the wind farms with instructions over the same wifi. This constitutes what Miss Mcintyre termed an air gap security model. Correct so far?"

Justin asserted, "Except it's not secure, but yes, that's right."

"Okay, then within each tower, there's an Ethernet switch that one, connects to all the other towers over a fiber optic ring and two, connects to a Microsoft Windows 2003 server?"

"Correct. One server per tower."

"And that Windows 2003 server both sends and receives information to and from the programmable logic controller that operates the entire structure, the turbine blades, the drive shaft, etcetera. And this occurs over a directly connected serial cable?"

"Right," said Justin, "and there's one more Win 2003 server for the entire wind farm, a controller that manages the power output to the generator. I didn't have time to capture that image, but I was able to hack into it as easily as the others."

"Okay, we'll discuss the systems next, but that's it for the data communications, right?"

"Yes, except for a discussion on the protocols involved. There are three. The radio system between the on-shore operations center and the boats is referred to as TETRA for terrestrial trunked radio. I'm not familiar with that, so I can't say what security concerns there might be."

Justin continued explaining the protocols. "Next is TCP over the Ethernet within the nacelle, the housing of the turbine, and across the fiber ring. That's a problem considering the wifi is unprotected. It's an open network.

"Last, the serial cable connecting the Windows 2003 server to the PLCs in each turbine uses a protocol called Modbus. An extremely simple request-response protocol without any authentication requirements. That's important to note for when we discuss the breach."

"Okay. Give me a second to add the protocols to this slide and we can move on to the next topic. I'll ask you to speak to the Modbus protocol Justin, if necessary. First time I've heard of it."

17

While Justin and Rob were equal partners in the firm, Rob was senior in terms of security experience. At fifty-five years of age, he had about fifteen years on Justin. Still, Rob's technical days were well behind him. He possessed the communication skills to deliver this presentation, but would need Justin to get into the weeds on data networking concepts.

Likewise, he would need K.C. to explain security concepts if necessary. She wasn't a partner, and was twenty-six years younger than Rob, but an expert on coding the algorithms that understood security intelligence. Her primary role on this trip was in automating Rob and Justin's pen test activities.

Rob updated his slide and moved to the next one. They worked on their presentation and delivery queues throughout the morning, then ate lunch in the hotel pub before walking to their client's offices for their 1 pm meeting. Like magic, the clouds evaporated, and while still a wet and cold 50°F, it felt good to Rob to get outside. *Tomorrow's hike is still on.*

***

Rob's client was a wind farm operations firm named Mistral Controls, a small subsidiary of Siemens - the German engineering conglomerate. The president wasn't available for the meeting, but it was led by Mistral Control's CFO Peter Wadsworth, the executive who signed their contract and was Claire's boss. The only four Mistral Controls employees present at the meeting were Peter and one of his staff members, a woman who appeared to be tasked with taking meeting minutes, and Claire with one of her staff members, a twenty-something-year-old who was the only one of the four not wearing a suit jacket. Rob judged him to perhaps have some IT skills based on his less formal appearance.

After clicking through his standard slides that set the agenda, reviewing the client environment since he couldn't be certain the CFO would already have the technical background, and explaining his team's methods and procedures, Rob began to detail their findings. His slides were simply bullet points. He didn't have to look at them as he went into story-telling mode. Bullet points don't tell a story, and it was the story that would leave a lasting impression with his client.

"Okay, let me reiterate our top findings. I think they're important enough to lead to a failed audit, and you'll want to take action." Rob did turn to scan these five bullets on his chart that were projected behind him on the wall, because he was setting up Claire to think this audit prep was the essence of his team's work. He was purposely giving her a false sense of confidence, to keep her from interrupting him too much.

"Finding number one is unprotected wifi on the wind farm. I have no doubt that some auditors might agree with Claire, that the other controls in place, namely the North Sea, would strongly mitigate the chance of this being a potential attack vector. But clearly, you've left your doors unlocked." Rob paused. Crickets.

"Understand what an APT is. Advanced Persistent Threats have several attributes. Advanced implies that a nation state, or some other entity with sufficient resources, will in fact, go out of their way and do whatever it takes to access your data. They will, in fact, send out a boat to scan your wind farm servers, if they made you their target."

Pause. Crickets.

"And by being persistent, they won't stop looking for your weaknesses. Once they've discovered your operations center isn't connected to the Internet, as part of your air gap defenses, their next step will be to boat out to the wind farm itself."

Pause. Crickets.

"So, this is more than a potential audit finding, this is a serious security lapse." Rob caught the scowl from Claire. She was very friendly up until now but he no longer expected her to escort him outside today, as she had the previous three afternoons.

"Next on the list, you're not running any file integrity monitoring software on the servers. Regulatory compliance specs are sometimes vague, but this is clearly called out. Logging isn't good enough because logs can be tampered with just like any other file. Especially when the logs are stored locally, as they are here."

Claire interrupted. "Rob, you seem to have missed the point of our air gap security policy. Without a connection to the Internet, or some type of always-on network connection, these servers can't forward alerts. They would have to queue the alerts until we collect the logs. So alerting software is really no different from any other log data, since it is not going to be real-time. And we regularly review our logs."

"Understood. And I know that to be your response to finding number three, that you aren't running Host Intrusion Prevention Software on your servers. At least HIPS could block potential threats automatically, even if it can't send alerts in real-time."

"Point taken, Robert." Claire wasn't overly concerned. She expected to be able to easily defend herself to Peter after these consultants had gone home.

"The last finding is minor in that it would not lead to failing an audit, but running Windows 2003 servers is seriously ill-advised. The known vulnerabilities are too great to count. We easily breached the server, and from there, we leveraged the Modus commands to take control of the function of the wind tower."

"Right," Claire interrupted again, ready to wrap this show up. "I want you to know Robert, I do take your findings seriously and I find your report extremely useful. And Peter, great timing on bringing in Robert's team as this will position us with ample opportunity to close these gaps in our security posture before our next audit. Well done."

"I have a few more slides, Claire." Rob wasn't finished. "Our forensics report, and then a list of recommendations."

"Oh. I thought the forensics was your rhetoric on the findings?"

"No. Forensics consist of another effort we perform to determine if there's been any compromise to your systems based on our findings. It's what my firm normally does for our clients, as opposed to performing penetration testing as we've done for Mistral Controls. We had enough time to conduct some preliminary forensics. I hope you appreciate it."

"I see. And have we been compromised, Robert?" Claire felt a flutter in her stomach.

"Well, this is as much art as science, but yes, I believe you have."

Claire, fortunately sitting at the table, felt a wave of nausea overtake her. She should have eaten more and drank less last night.

"This next slide is a display of twenty readings, recorded every thirty seconds by your system logs, from one of your servers. I don't have to present the other thirty-two servers because their readings are, for the most part, identical. The same logs have clearly been modified. I'll point this out. And you'll also see odd behavior in logs from the final hour before Justin collected them, that have not been modified. I'll point this out as well."

Rob gave his attention to Peter on this slide as he knew looking at Claire would not be constructive for this part of the presentation.

"The thirty-second entries, repeated on every row in these

modified logs, highlighted in light blue, are your wind speed measurements. Note they mostly read seven miles per hour. Some show six miles per hour, some are eight. The other readings from previous days are one hundred percent identical between servers. I've consulted with your system engineers and they've confirmed that correlation across the various servers for these other measurements tend to be quite strong, but they would never show one hundred percent correlation with previous day's logs. Ever. The dark blue readings are from the final hour and show only eighty percent correlation.

"Next, look at the pitch reading. These are highlighted in pink where they've been modified and are identical, but look at the red where they've yet to be tampered with. Pitch is oftentimes controlled by your software and modified, to optimize performance of the blades for the wind conditions. It might be reset a couple of times in a single day. Notice how this pitch is being modified every two minutes.

"Then look at the readings highlighted in dark green. These are the controlled speed of your turbines. These are sometimes controlled for strong winds to keep them from spinning too quickly and damaging themselves. They would never be controlled for mild, seven mile per hour winds. And again, note how they are being reset every two minutes.

"It's the same story for your power measurements. This entire system is being radically modified every two minutes, for the unmodified portion of the logs."

Peter, horrified of the potential answer, asked his first question of the meeting. "Robert, did you ask our engineers of the impact from these modifications?"

"I did, sir. They said there isn't real-world data to know with any specificity, but they would expect these modifications to result in two types of impact. A reduced mean time between failure from roughly a decade, to several months, on the turbines and some of the power components. Secondly, your power output efficiency would be dramatically reduced. They can't say by how much though because clearly the logs are being modified.

"Which is why we suspect we only see these anomalous recordings on the morning Justin collected the logs, even though he collected the previous forty-four days as well. The logs were modified to hide these actions, probably via a cron job that runs every hour. You'll note when I discuss recommendations that you should log remotely to mitigate the chance of such tampering.

"One last finding from my team back in Austin that analyzed these logs. They did a compare of a production image against your standard image and found a couple of encrypted files unique to the production image. These files are very likely the malware that's infected your servers. We can't say with any certainty because the files are encrypted, but we know they are not part of your standard server image. I would say your systems have been breached."

Peter asked, "Breached with what goal in mind? I can't imagine there being any value in their data."

"Right. This breach appears very similar to the StuxNet attack against Iran. That was an attack against the integrity of the centrifuges Iran employed in their nuclear program. Mean time between failure of the centrifuges was reduced to months if not weeks, dramatically slowing the pace of their uranium enrichment efforts. This is a system integrity slash denial of service attack against your energy production. The reasons behind that, well, I can only speculate. Could be industrial sabotage by a competitor."

"I see," Peter looked directly at Claire as he spoke to Rob. "Does your firm offer incident response services, Robert?"

"Yes, but not in-country. For the sake of urgency, I recommend you attain the services of a local firm. Although we've inferred the actions of those two files from reviewing the unmodified logs, have them run a routine to monitor the malware's actions. That'll be useful. I can email you my recommendations for a good local team."

"Please do," Peter said with his gaze still fixed on Claire.

***

Alone and drunk in her flat, Claire talked to herself as she researched the web on how to anonymously post the Americans' PowerPoint for sale. If some hacker group thought there was value in breaching their wind farm, maybe they'd be willing to procure the expert findings exposing their cyberattack. She thought about what the report might be worth as she read a Wikipedia article on how to access the dark web.

Okay, so step one is to run a VPN to obscure my IP address and physical location. Sounds like something I might want to do. I don't suppose I can use the Cisco VPN client I used for work anymore?

Claire googled the top ten, free VPN clients. She did this from her personal 13-inch MacBook sitting at her secretary desk, since her employer retained her work laptop after sacking her. She read good reviews for a free product called HotSpot Shield, downloaded and installed it. Took a couple of minutes. *Easy Peasy.*

She turned back to her Wikipedia article and read about using the TOR network. She got the part about TOR standing for The Onion Router, a U.S. Navy project decades earlier. She didn't understand the technical details describing how the data headers containing her IP address were encrypted and decrypted in layers, like an onion.

She generalized that explanation in her head to be similar to if Yodel or UPS delivered a package from the warehouse to her house by only looking at the street address of each next stop, from an Amazon warehouse in London, to the street address of the following delivery hub. That hub would use the street address of another delivery hub in her city, and only then would the driver in her town see the final street address of her house. Then somehow this would work in reverse.

Okay, I don't think I really need to understand all these details. Just give me a link to download the TOR browser. Claire found the link after scrolling further down. It led to a site where, after a couple of clicks, she was able to install a modified version of the Firefox web browser.

Easy peasy. Claire finished her glass of Malbec and headed to the kitchen to open a second bottle. She knew she was pissed and figured if she was found out, being drunk might serve as a defense.

Returning to her desk with the refilled wine glass in hand, she relocated her laptop to the living room couch to resume step three, researching how to sell something on the Dark Net. She first launched her Hot Spot Shield VPN client and TOR-enabled web browser to obscure her searches. Using the Duck Duck Go search engine to further obscure her tracks, she read through a query of top Dark Net marketplaces to post her PowerPoint for sale. She stumbled upon darkwebnews.com and learned a great deal before finishing her glass of wine. Next, she established a BitCoin account before heading for another refill in the kitchen. She poured this glass more fully to allow her more time to continue reading without interruption.

During this next round of research, she ended up on a Reddit site called DarkNetMarkets, where she learned which Dark Net marketplace might be best for her purposes. Eventually, she settled on the Alpha Bay Market and uploaded her file for sale. As she was auctioning this confidential file for both spite and financial gain, she listed her content for a hundred thousand pounds. It was a ballsy sum and she didn't expect any hits, but if this actually worked, she would be able to travel the rest of the year and not seriously begin looking for a new job until January. A part of her desired to be found out so that Peter would regret sacking her.

With the file posted, Claire returned to the kitchen for a third large pour from the second bottle of Malbec. She never made it to bed but passed out legless on her sofa after finishing the glass. She expected this to happen and, her drunken decision-making notwithstanding, slept satisfied with her evening's accomplishments.

Chapter Four

ANDREI was as dominant and aggressive as the next guy, but his favorite position with his model girlfriend, Danica Ivanova, was to let her ride on top.

She was so utterly gorgeous, the quintessential Macedonian beauty queen, as tall as him at five foot, nine inches, naturally tan skin, light brunette hair, with hazel eyes and a curvaceous body on top of long slender legs. He would be remiss not to watch her perform from below as they had sex.

The predominant theory was that Danica, a year older than him at twenty-two, wore the pants in their relationship. Not that she didn't appear youthful, but she could easily pass for thirty with the mature way she carried herself, while Andrei, with his pudgy baby face, would still sometimes be perceived as being younger than his eighteen-year-old brother.

He watched her artfully glide off after climaxing, and laid down without covering herself. Although his hotel room, which he permanently rented for his residence, had air conditioning, Danica insisted they leave the balcony glass doors open to feel the summer night air roll in off the lake as they sleep. He hated this. This July felt hotter than normal and August was expected to be more of the same. He rose naked from the bed to check his laptop screen for status on the Dark Web marketplace he operated.

Six new posts were waiting for his approval as moderator before the sellers could publish their wares in his marketplace. Five of them were staunches of stolen credit cards. Serving as a platform to sell stolen credit cards to *Carders*, the groups that were bold enough to actually go shopping with them, such uploads constituted ninety percent of his marketplace's revenue. He recognized the sellers and quickly approved them without conducting further research.

The sixth post blew him away. A new user, *Emerald Queen,* was asking for £100,000 for a single document on security audit findings for Mistral Controls. The amount was staggering enough, he could trade several million credit cards for that, but it was the content that had his mind racing.

Without approving the post, he bought it directly himself and then rejected it from being sold further. His Bitcoin balance was well over a million British pounds, thanks partly to the virtual currency market value increasing in his favor by eighty percent since the start of the year. Might as well spend it before the value crashed back down. Still, he'd have to delay purchasing that Tesla for Danica.

He downloaded the file after completing the Bitcoin transaction. It was a PowerPoint presentation, apparently drafted by some security consultants for the wind farm operation he hacked into over the winter. He quickly read through the thirty-plus slides, he only needed to scan the words to understand his stealthy compromise of their systems had been fully discovered. *Fucking unbelievable. I need to call the General.*

"Danica baby, I have some issues at work. I'm going to step out on the patio to make some calls."

"Shut down your laptop screen before you leave darling. The light bothers my eyes."

"Sure, baby."

Andrei closed the screen over his keyboard and stepped out onto his fifth-floor balcony, still completely nude, and phoned the Russian General of the GRU, Russia's Main Intelligence Directorate in their Ministry of Defense, while viewing the many boat lights over Lake Ohrid. Moscow was an hour ahead of Ohrid, but Andrei had a good relationship with the General and believed he wouldn't be overly aggravated by a call after midnight. Especially once he understood the gravity of their situation.

The General answered his secure mobile. "Andrei, this better be good."

"Sorry to wake you General, but you'll want to hear this. I just emailed you a file someone posted for sale on my marketplace for a hundred thousand pounds."

"I can see how that's good for you, given you take a percentage of sales. How is this something I want to hear?"

"I bought the file myself, General. It presents the findings by an American pen test team outlining our efforts at the UK offshore wind farm. They figured out quite a bit and I'm concerned this could compromise our larger project."

"You spent £100,000 without my pre-approval?"

"General, they've discovered the filenames of our attack code. They could warn the entire energy industry. At a minimum, there might be signature updates developed by the standard antivirus vendors to detect our exploits in another month. This adds a sense of urgency to our operation."

"I get that, Andrei. I'm just fucking with you." The General chuckled. "Still, don't submit that expense until September. Finances are tight."

Andrei smiled, appreciative of the General's generosity. He was worried about the £100,000. As a rule, Andrei didn't submit any expenses. He didn't get paid for the work he did for the General. It was expected of him to support cyber operations upon request for Mother Russia. In return, the authorities turned a blind eye toward his cybercrime activities - as long as they were directed toward Western countries - which were generally considered victimless crimes. They had an understanding that Andrei could submit expenses for reimbursement for extraordinary items, like when he had to travel to the UK and rent a trawler to hack into the offshore wind farm.

"I can give you a quick summary of the presentation, General. If you are not aware, a penetration testing team like this is hired by companies to try to hack into their networks so that they can report on vulnerabilities. There's no indication they were responding to an incident.

"They discovered our code by running a file compare against a clean server image. That exposed two of our files, the rootkit that controls the wind farm systems, and the file we use to rewrite the logs after the rootkit runs. Both files are encrypted, so all they really have is inference, but they listed the file names in their deck and they've made some spot-on conclusions."

"I see. Was this easy for them or are they good?"

"Well, you should know the owner of this firm, Response Software, is Robert Warner. You've maybe heard of him from last year's Black Hat counterattack against a casino-run, cyberwar operation?"

"I'm familiar with him, yes."

"They have some good tech. They forwarded the logs to a data scientist in Texas and that person did some fairly powerful data analysis using big data tools. Something called an ELK stack from Elastic Search. I've heard of it." Andrei considered how much he should delve into the weeds with the General.

"General, I don't say this in my email to you, but I think we need to act quickly. These Americans are consultants. They'll leverage this to win contracts with other firms in the energy industry. If that PowerPoint is worth £100,000, these consultants can't ignore the opportunity to pen test other wind farms."

"I see, Andrei. Thank you for sharing this with me. Well done. Good night."

***

General Alexander Volkov, Sasha to his friends, led the Russian military intelligence agency termed the GRU. Some cybersecurity firms also referenced the General's cyber operations as APT 28, for the 28th known Advanced Persistent Threat, which was identified by traces of similarity in its hacking code and methods. General Volkov would prefer to maintain a stealthier profile for his cyber operations, but then he was also sort of partial to the moniker Fancy Bear, that was yet another popular reference for APT 28. It afforded him a certain degree of celebrity among his peers who oftentimes presented him with little stuffed teddy bears as gifts. He placed the best ones on the bookcase behind his office desk.

The General reviewed the PowerPoint presentation in depth. He had level five fluency in both English and German, and wanted to gain a sense of this Robert Warner's expertise. *Maybe Cyber Command leveraged the private sector the same way he relied upon hackers like Andrei?* He forwarded the file to his staff working night ops and went back to sleep. He was woken less than an hour later, with a call from his night ops shift manager, a Lieutenant Colonel, advising him to take immediate action.

"Sir, the code has weak encryption. Andrei used RSA ciphers that the NSA is known to have broken, I could break it remotely. It is imperative we take steps to acquire the pen test team's laptops before they head home to America, because decryption on a workbench would only take a few hours for anyone with the right tech. Plus, their laptops might help me hack into their servers to erase whatever they have uploaded."

The General didn't need approval to authorize wet work, he'd contact his squad in London himself, per protocol.

"Thank you, Lieutenant Colonel. I'll get those laptops for you."

He wasn't going to sleep anymore tonight. Given the importance of this project to Putin, he'd have to update him first thing in the morning. Other Generals might fret over having to share bad news. Volkov considered it just another opportunity for visibility.

Chapter Five

NEITHER of Rob's team members was happy with his insistence of a 4 am departure for their hike, that was until they watched the sunrise over the North Sea at the trailhead. K.C. captured a selfie of the three of them before sprinting out well ahead on her own, affording Rob and Justin the chance to talk about the pending sale of their firm to Cyber Business International.

"We still on target Rob, to close the transaction next month?"

"August 11th, just two more weeks. This might be our last work assignment together Justin." Rob reminisced. "You know we've only known each other for less than a year?"

"Eleven months exactly," recalled Justin. "I can remember walking into your office last summer and meeting Greg, thinking what a prick."

"You guys have made a good team this past year. You've worked over a dozen deals together. Made us some good money."

"I have to give Greg the credit. I've been in learning mode the entire time. That guy knows security."

"Well, you both deserve a lot of credit. Your forensics have allowed our developers to stay home, out of the field. And it's their software, automating your forensics tactics, that's driving the valuation. Not our little consulting practice."

"So, we still talking a hundred million?"

"Actually, we just use that as an easy-to-reference number. The exact sum on paper right now is a hundred and thirty million. After taxes, the six of us should walk away with well over fifteen million each. That's early retirement for me, Justin. What are your plans?"

"I haven't told anyone yet, but Meagan and I remarried last Friday. We're back together as a family." Justin blushed a wide smile, clearly happy.

"That's fantastic, Justin. I'm so happy for you. Thinking of buying a new house together then?"

"Yeah well, I know she wants to move to France, to train with her old Olympic cycling team. They all moved there at the start of the summer. She was crushed that she couldn't join them. She still has sponsors, but she couldn't make it work with the kids. I plan to surprise her. Greg and I were there two months ago on that job in Montpellier and I've been communicating with a local realtor."

"She have a shot at making the Olympic team still?"

"Well, no, not likely. She's too old now, in her late thirties. But her team has some strong contenders. And really, in cycling, there's a lot more opportunity than just the Olympics."

"You speak French?"

"No, not even close. Meagan is maybe a level four in fluency. She's had the kids taking lessons for the last two years. I think she's been dreaming that this would happen for her someday. She doesn't know it yet, but I intend to make her dreams come true. That's the least I can do for her for not giving up on me after all these years.

"What about you, Rob? What are your plans? What does early retirement mean?"

"Well, as you know, I love mountain hiking. Sue and I just finished building an A-frame near Estes Park. We'll have the certificate of occupancy in another week or two. The plan was to move in there to finish out my career, which I thought might be another ten years. I intended to make some retirement income by leading tourists through Rocky Mountain National Park on hikes.

"I'm not going to need additional retirement income now though. I suspect we'll look into trading that A-frame for something a bit more upscale. We'll stay in Colorado, but I could see us moving down to Durango or Telluride. The San Juans are some of my favorite mountains. Until now, affording something on the slopes in Telluride was beyond my wildest dreams."

"Nice. Too bad K.C. didn't join as a partner. I imagine she'll quit working once she delivers her baby."

"Yeah, well Bill's working on negotiating retention bonuses for K.C. and a few others as part of the transaction. I just talked to him Sunday and he felt pretty confident he could get a six-figure sum for each of them if they agree to stay on at CBI for a few years. She'll do okay. She's not even thirty years old."

***

K.C. reached a small town along the coastal trail a good ten minutes ahead of Rob and Justin and waited for them outside a pub that was offering both lunch and breakfast. Five months pregnant, she considered ordering off both menus.

Rob could keep up with her but stayed back with the less fit Justin to bring him up to speed on the details of completing the sale of their firm to their previous employer. Two of their other four partners, Bill and Greg, were Rob's long-time friends who also worked at CBI previously. A third, Marco, was a friend of Greg that they partnered up with because he was already developing automation software. The final partner was Dylan Moore, who owned the Austin-based Response Software dev/ops team that was also working on security automation software. He was mostly a silent partner now with Marco taking over the role of lead software developer.

Bill was onsite with CBI's legal team working on closing the transaction while Greg was back in Austin managing the business. Rob would typically be doing that while Greg would be in the field, but Rob's had this Norfolk Coast Path on his bucket list for years. It was just as he imagined with wide open vistas of the ocean as the trail winds along the clifftops. He spoke to K.C. after he saw her sitting outside the pub.

"This place look good, or did you just stop at the first place you saw?"

"I googled the best pubs in this town last night. This place will fill up for lunch, and as you can see, they have a healthy breakfast crowd too. Justin, they've got your fish and chips, even during breakfast hours. I think this is our place."

"Lead the way."

The three of them over-ate like only Americans could. They headed back out to the trail for the three-hour return hike after filling up their water bottles.

***

Once again, K.C. led the men on the return to the trailhead. Full from over-eating, combined with her five-month-old fetus, she was only twenty or so yards ahead of Rob and Justin as they reached the high point on the cliffs, midway on their return. That it was a workday might explain why they saw very few other hikers, but she passed a pair of men hiking in the opposite direction at this midpoint.

She couldn't help but note their immense size. Something in their cadence suggested they might be military. She was Air Force herself and married to a major in the Air Force. She then noticed they weren't carrying any gear, not even water bottles. She got an odd vibe as they made room to pass her by splitting around both sides of the trail, allowing her to pass in the middle. *Who does that?*

Her fear was confirmed as she heard Rob and Justin both grunt loudly a few seconds later. K.C. turned at the noise to see the two men attacking them. In simultaneous actions, the further away attacker side-kicked Justin in the chest, launching him over the cliff, while the attacker nearest her punched Rob in the face and kicked him high in the chest, sending him backward over the cliff as well. They both then turned toward her.

The closer attacker charged forward as if to tackle her. He was huge, well over a foot taller than her five foot, seven inches. K.C. was no shrinking violet, or the stereotypical diminutive Chinese woman. One hundred and thirty-five pounds normally, with muscles finely honed from daily weightlifting and martial arts training. She was twenty pounds heavier now, five months into her pregnancy, but she didn't feel any loss of movement or strength as she assumed a defensive fighting posture.

Her attacker raised his arms to shove her with his overwhelming mass. With the cliff merely three feet to her right, K.C. deftly chopped her right fist into the outside of the man's outstretched left arm, blocking it inward, while sidestepping between him and the cliff. Her next lightening quick action was to punch the projecting knuckles of her left fist into the man's left temple. He stopped his movement, slightly drooping his head. He was stunned. K.C. detected his fogginess and understood it would be momentary, perhaps for only a split second. This was all the time she required to grab his left hand and elbow and with a well-practiced twist, she steered him toward the cliff, sending him over with a hard push in the back.

She turned back in the direction of the second attacker who had closed his position with her. Upon closer inspection, this attacker was actually a woman. Maybe. Her face had feminine features, her hair pulled back in a tight ponytail, and she appeared to have breasts. She was massive though for a woman, a slightly smaller version of her previous foe. She had stopped just out of kicking range, in front of K.C., and assumed a sideways fighting stance with her hands raised in front of her chin. Clearly, she assessed K.C.'s abilities and was being cautious before attacking.

There was no exchange of words. K.C. was also in a sideways fighting posture. She couldn't strike first because of the woman's advantage in arm length. She'd move inside after dodging the first blow. She didn't have to wait long.

The woman thrust her left fist at K.C's throat. K.C. was faster and blocked the jab with the same well-rehearsed move she employed against the first attacker, only instead of sidestepping right, she stepped in close with her right leg. The woman's second move was to raise her right knee into K.C.'s womb. K.C. countered this kick with her left knee, effectively blocking the attack. She quickly hooked the woman's leg with her left arm, holding it up, while blocking yet another left-hand side punch with her right arm. Her knee was still snagged on top of her attacker's raised knee. She freed it in time for the third blow, which she already knew would be a head-butt, because that was the best-leveraged appendage for this brick house to use at this close distance, with a leg and arm locked up by K.C.

Anticipating the head-butt, K.C. dropped her body to the ground with perfect timing. Her attacker's forward momentum carried her down on top of K.C., who planned to maintain the movement with a roll. This was the first act in this fight to go against K.C. as the woman's right knee, still hooked by K.C.'s arm, speared her hard in the left side of her abdomen. The interruption to her breathing nearly broke the roll, but K.C. willed herself to push the woman over her head with a twist toward the cliff.

The woman's legs and torso dropped over the cliff, but her shoulders and arms remained above. K.C., still on the turf and on her side, spun and kicked the woman with three quick successions in the face. The woman pulled K.C.'s right leg with her as she disappeared over the edge, releasing it almost as quickly as she fell, but not before K.C.'s legs were hanging over the cliff.

K.C. was not in danger of falling, but before she pulled her legs back up, she felt a hand grip her right ankle and heard a yell, "K.C.! Help!"

Chapter Six

K.C.'s husband, Major Calvert, walked up to the table while two privates stood guard by the closed door. He stared into Claire's eyes, sizing her up and hopefully instilling a sense of fear into her. He turned back toward the two privates and dismissed the shorter one. "Big Johnson, you stay." He then returned his stare back to Claire.

"Know why we call him Big Johnson, Ms. Mcintyre?"

Claire was slow to respond. She wasn't intimidated by men. She answered as if asking questions. "Because he's big? And because his last name is Johnson?"

"His last name is Meyers." Calvert paused long enough for the implication to sink in. "I don't normally sodomize my captives Ms. Mcintyre, but when I do, I like to use Big Johnson."

"You Americans are base."

"Base?"

"You're pigs!"

Calvert strode aggressively around the table and haunched over Claire, pulling her head back with a fistful of her short hair, hovering his face above her's by inches. He shouted at her like a drill sergeant.

"Pig? I assure you, Ms. Mcintyre, I'm a fucking wild boar! I'm a mad hog fixin' to rip your body into shreds!"

Spit flew from his mouth onto her face as he yelled. He paused for a moment and allowed a glob of saliva to drip from his mouth onto her upper lip.

"Your actions resulted in an attack on three Americans this morning. The three Americans whose report you sold last night online. One of them is now dead. And K.C., the pregnant woman, do you remember K.C., Ms. Mcintyre?"

Claire was now catatonic and no longer able to respond.

"K.C. is my wife you fucking whore. You're not leaving this room alive. Answer my questions, and I'll kill you quick. Do you understand me?"

At 6'0" and athletically trim, Calvert wasn't a huge man. His intimidation came from his intense, blue eyes. He could give a crazy look like Mel Gibson in the Lethal Weapon movies.

Claire was still unable to speak. Calvert knew he had her though, not from the tears welling up in her eyes, but by the sound of her pee dribbling down on the floor.

"Who did you sell that report to? Answer!"

Claire, feeling as if she'd already died, found her voice and stuttered, " I don't know. I listed it in an online auction. By morning, someone had purchased it. Just one purchase. They paid my BitCoin account anonymously. I don't know who they are. It's not possible to know other than their username."

"How much did they pay you?"

"A hundred thousand pounds."

"Are you kidding me? Someone paid one hundred thousand pounds for a PowerPoint?"

"I know. I should have asked for more."

Calvert was stunned by this last response. *This woman has issues.*

"What's the password to your computer?"

"Gr33nlight. Uppercase G and threes instead of the letter e." Claire cried this between sobbing breaths.

"What're your user credentials to the online auction?"

"I have a password file in my documents folder. Called recipes. It contains all my account information. It's not encrypted."

This sounded plausible to Calvert. He didn't know what else she could give him. He abruptly stepped back from her and walked toward the door.

"Private Meyers, thank you for your assistance. I'm finished here." He walked out the door with this last statement.

Claire presumed this meant Private Meyers had been left to have his way with her. She curled up in her chair, wrapping her arms around her shins, attempting to shrink into nothingness.

Private Meyers calculated the time for his replacement to show up. Seven minutes. If he could avoid having his commander walk in until then, he won't have to clean the mess Claire made on the floor. The private standing guard with him earlier reentered the room though, he'd forgotten about him. He instructed him to retrieve a mop.

***

After his interrogation of the only asset available to him so far, Calvert rejoined the British major assigned to him as an escort, in the curved hallway of GCHQ, the U.K. spy headquarters in Cheltenham. His escort picked up the conversation from where he'd left it earlier. He wanted details of the well-publicized cyberwar event Calvert was involved in the previous summer.

"Major, were you in command of Level 3 as they responded to Iran's DDoS attack against the world's major financial centers? How confident are you of their preparedness for the next cyberwar?"

"They rallied." Calvert wasn't sure of how straight-forward he cared to answer. "Major Fitzmaurice, I do indeed have extensive experience leveraging my resources in Level 3. My command of Level 3 staff was streamed online in real-time. So when you ask me of my confidence level, could you please be more specific, beyond the inherent respect I would feel for any other troops who carried the day?"

"I'll strive to convey myself more clearly for you, Major Calvert. Level 3 came across to me as in reactionary mode. Always one step behind the automation during last year's BlackHat. Not unlike most managed security solutions."

Major Fitzmaurice paused to recall the events from the six-day cyberwar Iran launched against Calvert, only a Captain then. Fitzmaurice remembered the only reason he thought of it as an attack against Calvert personally rather than the States was because of how perfectly Calvert leveraged his role as a Captain of the U.S. Air Force at a major tech conference into his own personal branding.

"Is it true then, Major? Did Microsoft offer you two million U.S. dollars to retire and join their LinkedIn business unit? Seriously mate. If you're ignorant to this massive opportunity…tell me. What is it you're thinking, Major Calvert? *Our world* is looking for leadership."

"Thank you for that, Major Fitzmaurice. Sometimes I forget." Calvert determined to keep his wits about him as he devolved into a nearly automated monolog on his self-announced Cyber War I the previous summer. *Has it only been twelve months?* He could typically fall half-asleep as he retold his worn story of leading a cyber counter-attack with major media channels looking over his shoulder. No cyberwar of any kind, between sovereign states, ever had that level of media coverage. Cyber Command had been booking him as a regular guest on the news networks ever since.

"Major, I imagine the magnitude of events in the States lose their amplitude as they stream across the ocean. I expect money to come at some point in my life, but I'm not focused on it. I'm certainly not waiting for it. Between you and me, Major, I can feel it coming. Until then, out of my many options, I choose to lead from the front lines. I'm not discounting corporate America in my future. I'm their biggest fan. Keep sending me troops, I like to say."

"So Cyber Command is taking care of you then?"

"You're very perceptive Major Fitzmaurice. There seem to be two camps of superior officers. Collectively of course, they promoted me to major, which I appreciated very much. But I will tell you that for the Generals who don't quite understand that we are in fact at war when it comes to cyber, very much like the cold war, it's a persistent adversary. They treat me like a Keurig coffee maker. I assume you have those over here?"

"I have one in my office. I like to show it off to my less sophisticated colleagues."

"Exactly. They like to show me off. Send me to speaking engagements. Put me in front of the media. I'm their Keurig." Calvert paused. "But the other half, and the ones who matter because they're in my direct chain of command, they give me assignments like what you and I will be partnering on next week. And for that I'm grateful."

"I'm not surprised by your decision to stay in the Service, Major. Well done. Tell me then, how can I help you in your mission this afternoon?"

"I need fuel to fly to the Lowestoft Hospital, somewhere north of here I'm guessing. I'm so tired right now Major, I honestly admit I have no idea of the cardinal points on this planet, relative to where I'm standing. I do know that I am headed to the North

Sea. I trust you can infer my leanings from that?"

"Indeed I can, Major. I was informed your F-14 Tomcat's petrol was refueled about ten minutes ago. Navy jet, right?"

"I can explain that. While I'm Air Force, Cyber Com is comprised from all the American military branches."

"And you flew without a co-pilot?"

"I was in a rush, Major."

"Well then Major, this feels somewhat presumptuous for me to say now, but I've already been instructed by Joint Command to commandeer both your jet and your calendar. You'll be my co-pilot as I fly you to the North Sea. Ready Major?"

"Have you flown a Tomcat before?"

"Two full weeks of flight time. Three years ago. I trust you'll chirp at me when I need direction?"

"Point the way."

***

Calvert walked into the James Paget Hospital while Fitzmaurice parked the car. Their flight went quickly with Fitzmaurice briefing Calvert on everything his unit learned during the day about his wife's attackers. It was a small hospital and he found his wife without delay, as Fitzmaurice already staffed the building with guards, in a private room in the emergency center. Her eyes were resting as he entered the room.

"You awake, darlin'?"

"Jamie! It's still Friday. How'd you get here so fast?"

"It's barely Friday still, but yeah. I got here as fast as I could. I haven't talked with the doctors yet baby. Are you okay?"

"I'm fine, honey. Baby's fine too. Close call though. I bruised my kidney, as if my kidneys weren't under enough pressure already."

The long day and stress erupted from Calvert in sobbing tears after hearing the baby survived. He buried his head into his wife's hair and pillow to cover his crying. Fitzmaurice walked in at that moment, and quickly exited.

"Let it out, honey. I had a good cry myself after the doctor told me our diagnosis."

Calvert recovered his composure, kissed the side of her head and stood back up to talk. "Do you know about Justin then too?"

K.C.'s face scrunched up and shed a tear as she responded. "Oh yes. I just can't believe it, Jamie. We had breakfast this morning at the cutest little pub you could imagine, along the coast. He just remarried his ex-wife last weekend. That poor woman. Who's going to tell her?"

"I wish I could do it. It's not my place though, and I'm not going to be headed back any time soon. I understand Rob's fine, minor injury to his abdomen."

"Yes, I haven't seen him since we arrived. I don't think he's walking yet. We shared the ambulance ride. We both want answers, Jamie. This can't possibly be related to our pen test for Mistral Controls?"

"I believe it is. Their CISO, Ms. Claire Mcintyre, sold your presentation on the dark net last night."

"That bitch."

"Oh, she's a piece of work," Calvert continued. "It's hard to fully understand the motive. I mean, why kill over this, unless it's much bigger than just this one wind farm? Your attackers are attached to the Russian Embassy in London. We have countless video feeds of them entering and exiting. The bobbies got that much.

"I had the Intelligence Branch of the Royal Air Force take over as soon as I was made aware. They followed up with a third embassy staffer seen in some of the same videos with your attackers. The bobbies couldn't get anywhere with him, diplomatic immunity and whatnot, but the Air Force is treating this as a military act of aggression.

"They ID'd your attackers as Russian military. GRU. And if this is related to the compromise you discovered on the wind farm, then this is an ongoing cyberattack. They raided the third Russian and recovered your laptops. We're not allowed to detain him for interrogation, but CCTV proves he stole them from your hotel while you were on your hike. I need to see your forensics behind the PowerPoint. What's your password, darlin'?"

"Little Private Calvert. Uppercase L, P, and C, 1s for the i letters and 3s for the e characters. But I don't have any of the forensics. I was coding algorithms to automate Justin's pen test actions. Get with our intern, Sara. She did the work on that, back in Austin. I do have the PowerPoint presentation though. That will give you the background."

"Good. I'm going to have to travel to GCHQ in Cheltenham to view that. And I'll follow up with little Sara. I'm sorry I can't stay longer, darlin'. Will they be letting you out soon?"

"Tomorrow, I think."

"I'll have my men here by then. They'll take you to my hotel in Cheltenham. Once I have one. I'm going to stop by to check in on Rob. I love you, darlin'."

"Love you too, Jamie. You seem to be close to your English counterpart?"

"We've been spending some time together lately. That's all I can say. Goodnight, darlin'."

***

Rob's door was also guarded by the Royal Air Force.

"You awake, Mr. Warner?"

"Why wouldn't I be? It's a hospital. I was just thinking of giving you a call, Major Calvert. Come on in."

"Glad to see you're in good spirits, Mr. Warner. I just came from K.C.'s room. She and the baby are doing fine."

"Well, that is good to hear. Thanks for sharing that with me. This a personal visit or business?"

"Both, and now that we've got the personal visit out of the way, let's talk business," Calvert said with a smirk as the two of them enjoy the rapport they developed since first meeting a year earlier on an international cyber attack that brought a degree of celebrity to them both.

"I understand I should debrief little Sara to better understand what ya'll found at Mistral Controls?"

"I'm not sure she understands what she discovered. My PowerPoint lays it all out fairly well. But she's also had a full day now so she might have uncovered more intel. You headed to Austin next?"

"No. I'm having her transported out here to the Doughnut, so I won't be breaking any of the European data privacy laws you likely did when you forwarded logs to her across borders."

"Justin did that," Rob responded sheepishly.

Calvert lost his conversational momentum momentarily, digesting how Rob just threw his recently deceased business partner under the bus.

"I expect to quickly have an endless supply of wind farm server logs for someone to busy themselves with. No need to supply her with a corporate credit card. The tab will be on me."

"That will be an awesome experience for her. Thank you, Major.

Can you tell me anything about our attack?"

"You think you have a need to know?"

"Just trying to help, Major."

"You can help by answering my questions."

"I could help more if I had some context. If those attackers really were after us intentionally, how'd they know we'd be on that trail? I shared with Claire and Peter that we'd be hiking the Coastal Trail, but I didn't say what trailhead. It's a long trail. And why kill us? Wouldn't they do better to interrogate us?"

"They already had your information, Mr. Warner. Ms. Mcintyre sold them your PowerPoint presentation on a darknet marketplace last night for a hundred thousand pounds."

Rob's mouth dropped open.

"And they stole your laptops from your hotel while you were out hiking. They could have discovered your hiking plans from Justin's FaceBook page. He pretty much laid out all the details."

"Goddammit."

"They might have wanted to kill you to erase your knowledge of the breach."

"Mistral Controls knows."

"And how long do you think they would sit on it?"

"The European Energy Commission publishes guidelines for data breach notification that might give them weeks if not months. The pending GDPR guidelines will give them seventy-two hours when enacted next year. They might follow that now. I emailed Bill a business justification last night for the immediate hire of European pen testers to tap the energy industry for when this becomes public."

"They might go after them, but not right away. My wife just deactivated what are possibly their only in-country assets. Ms. Mcintyre is locked up. We can put a watch on their other key personnel."

"K.C. is one helluva badass, Major. She saved my life."

"What exactly happened?" Calvert saw Rob as being remarkably fit, about a hundred and eighty pounds and just under six feet in height, but also understood that at fifty-five he was no fighter. Rob, while healthy, was more of what you would expect of a man with half-gray hair and bifocals, a mature businessman.

"We were on our return, about halfway back. Incidentally, about the only spot where the cliffs are high enough where a fall would be certain death. Justin and I were walking side by side. K.C. was maybe twenty yards ahead of us. They were standing there until they saw us, then started hiking toward us. They passed K.C., and as soon as they reach Justin and me, they pushed us toward the edge, then punched and kicked us until we went over. It took basically one shove to position me, one punch to my chin to stun me senseless, and one kick to send me over."

"So you went over the cliff too?"

"I did, but a tree root snagged my belly a few feet down. It tore into me like a knife and held me there by my ribs. I started climbing back up, walking sideways along a small ledge. Before I knew it, the other two attackers fell over my head. Each time they almost took me with them. Then K.C.'s legs were dangling in front of my face. I literally climbed up over her. Wanna see my wound?"

"Sure."

Rob pulled down his blanket and peeled back the gauze over his gash.

"Those are some expert stitches. Still, that's going to leave a nasty mark. You never cease to amaze me, Mr. Warner. Trouble seems to find you, and you respond in kind."

Rob didn't reply but took it as a compliment as he covered himself back up.

"That's not totally a compliment, Mr. Warner. I want you staying away from this. When will you be released?"

"I expect tomorrow. Sunday at the latest. I think they're just watching me for infection."

"Okay then. I'm fine with you expanding your business opportunities around this, although CyberCom will take over the forensics at Mistral Controls. This will be over before you interview your first candidate. I want you on the first plane out of the U.K. Understood?"

"Understood, Major."

"Good. Now tell me who you think is behind this, Mr. Warner."

"I was talking to Greg an hour earlier. He said it's fair to consider the Lazarus Group, North Korea, because they've been focusing lately on Critical Infrastructure. But they are also very profit-oriented and focused even more on Bitcoin attacks. Plus, this appears to be sabotage. That rules out quite a few groups actually. He can't think of any hacktivists interested in destroying clean energy, at least not any with this sophistication. So that leaves us with nation states. His money is on Russia. We need to decrypt the files to look for signatures. We don't have the tech for that."

This last sentence was really a question for Calvert, as in how long will it take his team to decrypt the malware.

"I haven't seen the files yet. It will depend on what ciphers were used. There's no guarantee, but I can tell you that a team in Cheltenham is already on it."

Rob and Major Calvert's conversation drifted back into personal topics.

"So tell me, Mr. Warner, how would you evaluate the nursing at this British hospital?"

Rob had known Calvert a full year and shared with him a close friend and colleague, Greg Foyer. Greg was Rob's partner and an ex-military buddy of Calvert. Still, Rob struggled to accurately read Calvert's intentions, never quite certain when he was being serious. Calvert could be asking Rob for his evaluation of medical care in this single-payer country, but he recalled that his personal fetish for women in uniforms was revealed to Calvert during a fly-fishing trip. Hard to totally remember through the fog of strong Colorado craft beer, but he sensed Calvert was asking him his take on the local nurses' uniforms and offered up his opinion.

"Well, I've only had male nurses attend to me so far. I suspect they work twelve-hour shifts and have only had two men come into my room, not counting the doctors, both women by the way and old enough to be my grandmother. I'm hopeful I'll be able to report back more useful intel to you later, Major. I can tell you now though that the bobbies are quite darling in their little striped ties and hats."

"I was referring to the quality of care Mr. Warner, as my wife is also a patient here, but that's good to know. If it helps to keep up your spirits," Calvert lied, "the hallway is swarming with attractive female nurses wearing knee-length, white dress uniforms and smart hats. Get well Mr. Warner, I have to leave."

***

Minutes after Calvert left the room, Rob received a call on his mobile.

"Rob Warner."

"Mr. Warner? This is Nigel, the systems engineer from Mistral Controls. You asked me to review some server logs yesterday."

"I remember. How can I help you, Nigel?"

"I told you I'd continue researching other logs to see if I could find anything that would correlate to the power output your logs showed. I found billing records that suggest we've been generating anomalous power output from the wind farm for the last six months. The reports don't show the half-minute log intervals, or even two minutes to map to the breach pattern, but their daily numbers are noticeably down from corresponding months for the last two years. I'm surprised Finance hasn't already looked into this."

"That is interesting. You should share that with Peter Wadsworth. He's your CFO."

"I emailed Mr. Wadsworth already on it, but here's the thing. I contacted a friend of mine who works for a much larger operation in Germany. He discovered the same pattern in his server logs. Like us, he only saw the two minute changes in the last hour of today's partial logs. Clearly, earlier logs were modified. Then he checked his billing records. His pattern of lower wind farm revenues goes back ten months. And he's seen a notable increase in the number of turbines needing repairs this month. He asked me if you'd be willing to review his servers, you know, to look for malware. He'd like to keep this quiet while he's in a data discovery mode."

"Be happy to. He say when?"

"Monday, if that's not too soon. He has ten percent of his operations currently under repair."

"Ping me his contact info. I'll see what I can do."

Rob called his partner Greg next, with instructions to get on a plane.

Chapter Seven

SARA was hungry.   She barely arrived home after work Friday when a military Humvee parked outside.   Two good-looking men, whom Sara thought could be models, in fatigues, exited, walked up to her door, and explained to her mom how they were taking her to the U.K. to work with Major Calvert.   Her mom called her dad, who just got off the phone with Calvert, then helped her pack. Sara missed dinner.

The two nice looking soldiers drove her to Lackland Air Force Base in San Antonio, where she boarded a small passenger jet for a flight to somewhere in Georgia, where she boarded yet another plane, described to her as a C-130 cargo jet, that flew her to RAF Fairford Airbase, somewhere northwest of London.

It was now Saturday morning, and she was being driven by yet more very fine looking soldiers to what they called the Doughnut, a half hour more northwest in Cheltenham. Sara had yet to eat. She didn't know the difference between jet lag and low blood sugar, but she was confident she could ride out the jet lag if she could get some food. Sara also wondered if the military had some synthetic printer running off copies of these darling soldiers.

"Are we driving to breakfast?"   Her brain starved of glucose, Sara had already forgotten the two soldiers' names. She didn't care which of the two boys sitting up front answered.

"We've already eaten breakfast ma'am, but I'll inform the Major of your request."

"Bless your heart. Thank you."

Ma'am. These boys must have five years on me. Lordy, they're cute. Sara had yet to express much interest in boys at school, but traveling with these military men kindled something inside her. *They must think I'm older?*

The soldiers didn't talk unless spoken to and Sara was too tired for words. After driving through the English countryside for twenty minutes, on what she understood to be highway A417, much like a Travis County highway but without shoulders, they reached the city of Cheltenham. They parked in front of a large building. She gathered, more from the curve of the parking lot than from what she could see of the building itself, that it was round. Assuming it had a courtyard, she got the doughnut moniker.

The soldiers bypassed the security turnstile and took her to a side office where they printed her out a badge with a photo worse than any she'd ever taken. *Any.* She tried to put it in her backpack, but they handed her a lanyard and instructed her to wear it around her neck. They emphasized the importance of keeping the photo-side visible.

"Miss Thomas. I heard you were in the building. How was your flight?"

Sara raised her head after donning her lanyard to see Major Calvert standing in the doorway of the small office.

"Hello, sir. Mr. Calvert."

"You can call me Major, Miss Thomas. It's been a full year since we met at BlackHat. It's good to see you."

"Thank you for the job, Major. It's been really awesome."

One of the privates addressed Calvert. "Sir, Miss Thomas expressed an interest in having breakfast on our drive from Fairford."

"Well, of course, we can have breakfast." Calvert already ate but suspected more food might aid his own jet lag. "When's the last time you ate Miss Thomas?"

"Bless your heart, Major. Not since lunch yesterday. Military planes don't have flight attendants."

"No Miss Thomas, they don't. I'm so sorry about that. Let's address this right away." Calvert looked back at the private. "Her badge ready to go?"

"Yessir, her authorizations you requested are active, sir"

"Fine, thank you Private." Calvert returned his attention toward

Sara. "Miss Thomas, we could eat in the doughnut cafeteria, but think about how that sounds while we walk outside. I know a place where we can get you a proper English breakfast." Calvert had already worked four hours and would like a break from the building himself.

"Private, drive us to the Bayshill Inn on St Georges Place. Take the A40 to Lansdown."

"Yessir. May I suggest the Princess Elizabeth Way to A4019?"

"No thank you, Private. I'm going for sites over speed. Let's drive past the Ladies College."

"Yessir."

Ten minutes later, Sara found herself seated at an outdoor picnic table with the major somewhere in what she figured to be the town's center. She ordered a tuna and brie omelette with potatoes while the major ordered sausage and mash. Not one to assume a young girl with such a diminutive size couldn't have a healthy appetite, Calvert also ordered a fish and chip board as a starter, to be eaten if needed. Sara didn't begin to speak until the chip board arrived and she had a few bites.

"Wow, these are good. Sitting outside here is nice. It'd be too hot in the Hill Country, this late in the morning."

"I know. I mostly work in San Antonio. Maximizing your time in the sun will help you with jet lag. I've always had good results from eating too." Calvert grabbed his first bite after sensing Sara provided him an opening.

"I really want to thank you again Major for the summer job. But I can't imagine how I can help you. I barely know anything."

"Straight to business, Miss Thomas. Okay. First, you have experience in analyzing the system logs from wind turbines. Second, in the ELK stack, which seemed to have worked nicely for your analysis yesterday. And third, in querying a massive data lake of vulnerabilities and exploits that your firm maintains. Any idea how they put that extraordinary database together in such a short time?"

"I can't talk about that stuff, and honestly Major, I'm just learning how to use the ELK stack. I mean it's not terribly difficult. It's hardly something that takes ten thousand hours to become an expert."

"There's more, Miss Thomas. My team is already engaged in other projects. You're additional head count. Your skills might seem niche to you, but they are perfectly suited to the task at hand, and you'll require zero training time. Time is at a premium just now."

"Not that it isn't really cool to be here sir, but why not have me query logs from Austin?"

"I don't expect you to be overly familiar with international data privacy laws Miss Thomas, but trust me, Europe invented them. I had Jen, I believe she's your lead, transfer an instance of your AWS data lake to an offnet data center here in the U.K. In addition to playing by the rules, it affords us a measure of security should we lose trans Atlantic Internet connectivity to North America."

"Seriously?"

"It's a definite possibility. Should cyberwar break out, we'd be remiss not to have contingencies for that. A classic defensive tactic we call compartmentalizing systems."

Calvert had underestimated potential strikes in the past. He was running this exercise by consulting a physical playbook every four hours in a stand up meeting with his NATO counterparts. Not unlike facilitating an incident management and response plan after a breach.

"Can you tell me what an offnet data center is, sir?"

"Back at the Doughnut, you'll be assigned to a work bay with two workstations. One is connected to the Internet. You'll need that to download log files from several dozen wind farms where we've already established user access for you. You'll transfer files to a USB drive which you'll use to load the files into your second workstation. That computer is not connected to the Internet. Hence the term, offnet. It's connected to a military network where your new data lake has been instantiated. Jen worked through the night with my team here to rebuild your data lake and toolsets. She didn't have it finished until you arrived. You think you're tired."

The seriousness of this adventure began to dawn on Sara. She wasn't intimidated but rather so excited, she mentally directed any self-doubt to take a back seat to her enthusiasm. She stole the last fish slider when Calvert wasn't looking and scooped up the remaining tartar sauce.

"Oh, I think that's our food coming. Phew, I started thinking this place was slow."

***

Rob, still in his industrial hospital bed, had just completed purchasing a flight to Leipzig and was preparing to purchase a train ticket to Halle, when K.C. bopped into his room. He always considered her to be a beautiful woman, and he felt her pregnancy was making her flat Chinese cheeks more full, causing her face to shine even brighter.

"Rob, thought I'd say goodbye. They checked me out just after lunch."

"Good to see you doing okay, K.C. Since we got here, you never call. You never write."

"They run this place like a prison, Rob. They wouldn't let me get out into the hallway to walk around."

"Same here, although I intend to this afternoon since I just discovered I'll be spending another night."

"Oh, sorry to hear that. I was thinking there might be a chance of you sharing my ride to Cheltenham. Military escort. I'm sure the major would like to see you."

"The major stopped by here yesterday for a chat. What did we get ourselves into, K.C.?"

"Apparently, we're dangerously close to an all out cyberwar with Russia."

"Russia? You know that for sure?"

"Yes. Our attackers have been identified as working for the GRU. Russian military intelligence. The major didn't tell you that?"

"He asked me who I thought was behind it. He didn't share with me that he already knew."

"Oh, well then I probably shouldn't have told you that either. What do you think of the nurses here, Rob? I've had a couple of real sweethearts. Both my age, and so cute with their accents and little outfits. I'm already friends on Instagram with some of them."

Rob didn't respond other than to nod his head, and wondered privately if it would be possible to update his profile at this place.

"Did they tell you when you can expect to go home?"

"The doctor said first thing tomorrow morning. That I could even pre-checkout tonight. Just a formality to watch me for infection for so many hours before releasing me."

"I hope you don't mind if I take the week off to stay in Cheltenham? I might even do some work from there."

"Oh, for heaven's sake, no K.C. Take the week off. This has been nuts, you need to rest and try to absorb all this. I might take some time off too."

K.C. felt she maintained a father-daughter relationship with Rob. Rob thought she was pretty, but she was also only a few years older than his daughter, Ella. He hired her a year earlier after working together to counter a cyberattack that her previous firm, a casino, was involved in.

"You should, Rob. Have that pretty wife of yours join you out here."

"Maybe I'll do that." Rob looked into K.C.'s eyes before continuing. "K.C., I'm not sure if I even know where to begin apologizing."

"What do you mean?"

"I made you and Justin go on that hike. Like some cranky old scoutmaster."

"Oh Rob, don't do that to yourself. If we weren't attacked on those cliffs, it would have been somewhere else. You didn't get Justin killed. This is Russia. They're up to something. We're collateral damage, in the wrong place at the wrong time."

"Thanks for saying that. Enjoy your military escort."

"I will. Get better."

As K.C. exited the room, Rob purchased two train tickets from Leipzig to Halle. He'd connect with Greg, Sunday morning at the airport in Leipzig, and they'd ride the train together to Halle to prep for their meeting on Monday morning with their potential new client.

***

Calvert walked down the hallway of the Doughnut with a broad smile on his face. He just came from eating Sunday breakfast with his beautifully pregnant wife K.C. She joined him the previous night, and it was almost as if they were enjoying the honeymoon they never had, after marrying the week of Christmas, the previous year. He was headed for his first standup meeting of the day when his secure mobile rang. The call was from Captain Jefferies, a close confidant whom Calvert had been promoting right behind himself for a number of years.

"Major Calvert. Looks like they beat us to the first punch. The Automated Clearing House reported massive fraudulent online ACH transactions two hours ago. Which, being the middle of the night, I don't suspect they need very sophisticated algorithms to detect the unexpected volume."

"Give me a readout, Captain."

"I engaged our boys over at the major telcos, and have been working with them since to repurpose their Distributed Denial of Service mitigation infrastructure to detect and block the fraudulent transactions. Most of the transactions are hitting Amazon, which is their customer, so they've diverted ACH transactions to their Arbor boxes for detection. They had to write custom rules for BGP Flowspec, but ACH transactions are pretty simple. And we've identified most of the source IPs. That's harder, the source addresses are fairly dynamic, but the telcos are black-holing them as soon as they pop up."

"Who else besides Amazon?"

"The other end of the transactions were compromised personal bank accounts, and of course Wells Fargo was spoofed as the transaction originator. The telcos are leveraging Arbor appliances at their Internet POPs to detect transactions. They're at a point where they're blocking ninety-five percent of the transactions, so we're out in front of this. Next step is unwinding the transactions. That could take all week, sir."

"What was the volume of transactions?"

"Over a billion, sir. Nearly a month's worth of transactions in two hours. Amazon thought it was Black Friday. The telcos proposed using their Radware scrubbers on the NetFlow logs to automate reversing the transactions. That'll help speed things up, if it's even doable. It's an unconventional approach not supported by the vendor. I expect to be on this all week, sir."

"Tell me why and who, Captain."

"Oh, we haven't had time yet to perform forensics, sir. Geolocation suggests the Baltics, but that's clearly been spoofed. I think we can presume Russia, since it's typical for them to spoof the Baltics. It's just not clear to me why. There's no opportunity for financial gain here sir, just sowing chaos and keeping us busy."

"Thank you, Captain. Ping me hourly updates."

Calvert hung up as he walked into his standup briefing with his NATO peers. He stepped up alongside Fitzmaurice. Everyone in the room remained standing - the idea was that standing would help keep the meeting short. Conversation had yet to start and Calvert simply launched into it by sharing his phone call from Jefferies.

"The U.S. Financial system was attacked two hours ago with a first-of-a-kind DDoS. Being an FOAK attack, I don't know that I can even call it a DDoS - I'm taking liberties. The telcos have crafted a custom response with their DDoS mitigation infrastructure. Too early to say it was from Fancy Bear, but it's so innovative, it's definitely a Russian actor."

Fitzmaurice was the first to comment. "A DDoS attack outside of business hours? The U.S. is still in bed, Major."

"I'll give you the readout. You categorize it.

"If you're not familiar with the American ACH system, ACH stands for Automated Clearing House. It's a network for conducting electronic financial transactions, for everything from direct deposits to social security payments. It handles over twenty-five billion transactions each year, valued in the tens of trillions of dollars.

"This system is so transparent, with routing numbers and checking account numbers essentially public, but it's also completely authenticated. Only banks can initiate transactions. Americans think they transact directly with Amazon with their debit cards, but they don't. ACH is in the middle, settling the transactions. Bad transactions are easily reversed. This network has been in operation for decades.

"Two hours ago, over a billion fraudulent online transactions began hitting Amazon and other retailers. It was detected immediately and, because of the traffic volume, and other characteristics, it's being countered with DDoS mitigation techniques. I can't really say this is a DDoS, could be aimed at system integrity as much as availability. I haven't had time to consider how else to categorize this attack. It would help to know the motive."

Responses came from the room.

"You said fraudulent transactions are easily reversed?"

"Well, not a billion of them at once."

"What's the impact to your team, Major?"

"My Baltic attack team will be tied up for the next half week responding to this."

"That could very well be their objective."

"These Ruskies know hybrid warfare."

"They invented it."

"Well we are *Full-spectrum* cyberwarfare gentlemen, stay focused," Fitzmaurice corrected the room. "I can second my resources to your command, Major," he directed toward Calvert. "Might even speed up our launch time by a day since my troops are already here. Which we might need to. My team spoiled an attack by another two Russian operatives at 0300 against the Mistral Controls CFO. He's responsible for making the breach public next week. Whatever is planned, its launch is imminent."

"Brilliant Major, thank you."

The sound-baffling walls, in a room full of captains and majors, absorbed the vocals of readouts in a clockwise direction. The discussion ended with a survey of higher-up approvals for their plan to counter-attack Russia.

They didn't have a one hundred percent confirmation that Russia was the source of the breach, or that there was even a larger cyber event at play. Evidence from other vectors though suggested Russia was launching a cyberattack against European energy resources. It was not clear to the NATO officers why Russia would do this. An Estonian major lectured the room professorially on the topic.

"It's probably as simple as redirection via hybrid warfare while they make a land grab somewhere in Eastern Europe. This has been Russia's MO since Putin's been in power. Popular thought in the Media is that Russia attacks their sovereign neighbors out of national security concerns. Some in Academia suggest Russia is still searching for its Eurasian identity. Russia first gained a sense of self after being organized by Genghis Kahn into a Mongol-Turkic state, from the 13th to 15th centuries. Peter the Great turned their focus toward Europe, and they've had a Western-centric worldview ever since.

"The current thought leaders in Russia are behind a Eurasian movement, not unlike some of the nationalist trends in the West, that promotes disregard for the consequences of attacking Western neighbors as they establish their still-forming, nation-state identity, independent of East or West. I would tell you that Putin is leveraging that national sentiment to execute an acquisition plan supporting horizontal integration for his oil enterprise. He's eliminating the taxes his neighbors impose on his energy distribution network. It's just business."

Calvert interjected, "So, Russia doesn't like not being the center of a round globe. You know, there's not that many of them. Economically, their only relevance is oil and gas. I think we could take 'em."

Coincidentally, the stand-up dispersed based on the absence of speaking that followed Calvert's bizarre statement. The Estonian major pulled Calvert aside with a tap on his arm.

"I've been eager to speak with you Major, on your so-called cyberwar last year. I'm Major Jaan Sepp."

"Of course, Major. Good to make your acquaintance."

"When you declared last year's attack to be the very first cyberwar, I assumed you weren't aware of our Estonian cyberwar in 2007?"

"That thing over the little bronze statue? Yes, Major, I might have been in college when that occurred, but I am aware of it."

"Well then, you should also have known that we termed it the very first cyberwar. Cyber War I is how we reference it in Estonia. All of Europe recognizes that."

"All of Europe, Major? Maybe the Baltic States." Calvert was annoyed now. *Some guys just love to argue.*

"I'll tell you what, Major Sepp. If our plans escalate significantly beyond our expectations, I'll go on television and declare Estonia as ground zero for Cyber War II. But it's too late to erase the media generated from Cyber War I in Vegas last year. After that, I doubt your little bronze statue affair ranks very high in the google search results for cyberwar."

"I'm not trying to say this is a competition, Major. Perhaps you misunderstand me?"

Calvert was done with this chit-chat.

"Perhaps it's your accent?"

Major Sepp recognized the change in Calvert's tone. Nearly a half meter taller than Calvert, he was not afraid to launch into a fistfight with him in the hallway of the Doughnut. But he also recognized the warrior inside of Calvert. He saw the sudden viciousness in his eyes. Rather than test him, Sepp determined to respect him. It was good to see such feisty attitude among senior commanders. Looking forward to their future joint mission, he diffused the situation, that he admitted to himself he started, with humor.

"I speak American with a midwestern accent. By your drawl, I'm guessing you're from Texas." He completed his response with a wink and Calvert smiled.

"Native. San Antonio."

The two of them walked to lunch together.

***

Rob arrived at the Leipzig-Halle airport hours before Greg and was on the phone with his wife Sue, and eating lunch at an airport pub that overlooked the bahn terminal below.

"Sue, please, don't come out. I'm fine, and really, I'll be home probably tomorrow. Wednesday at the latest. I just don't want to book my flight until I meet the client and scope this project."

"I don't see direct flights from DIA. Bunch of one hops through either Frankfurt or Munich. Ooh, there's one through Paris on Norwegian Air for $346 one-way. But that won't help our Maui points."

"Doesn't surprise me but did you hear me when I said don't come out here? I'll be home in a couple of days."

"What hotel?"

"The Dormero Hotel Halle, but honey…"

"They don't have a Hilton in Halle? We need more points for Maui."

"It's located a few blocks away from a Beatles Museum. I couldn't pass that up."

"All work, hmm? I'll change that."

"Honey, please don't fly out here."

"Ella's on the other line dear. You know I have to get that. I'll bring you up-to-date on your daughter when I forward you my itinerary." Sue hung up.

"Dammit." Rob looked up to see Greg walking toward his table, having spotted him. At 6'2" and a skinny 180 pounds, Greg was hard to miss, especially with his Abe Lincoln-sized head. He was thirty years old but could pass for sixteen. "Greg. Guten tag."

"Guten tag, Herr Warner. That bruise on your face from the attack?"

"Yeah, that's nothing. I'll show you my stitches later at the hotel."

"Cool."

"I appreciate you dropping everything to come out, Greg. This going to delay our 3.0 code drop?"

"No, we're good. Marco left the negotiations in Boulder to lead the development effort in Austin."

"Good call. You wanna catch a bite here? We have another hour before our train departs."

"I'm stuffed. I could drink a local brew though." Greg dropped his travel bag and sat down.

"It's not noon yet."

"It's not 4 am for me yet."

"Hmm, it's a quick serve concept. I'll get us a couple of pints."

Rob returned after a few minutes with two dark-colored pints that he described as locally crafted lagers. "Cold-brewed in town, so they tell me."

"In memory of Justin." The two men clinked their pint glasses together and took a somber sip. After a few moments of silence, Greg asked, "Who we meeting with tomorrow?"

"Stephan Franke will greet us initially. He's an engineer in the ops center of a vast wind farm operation in Halle. He told me he'll introduce us to some managerial types. Hopefully, so we can sign a contract to perform an assessment around their Windows servers. There's a good chance we might find what we just discovered in the U.K."

"I wrote a script on the flight that will crawl their network looking for those two file names. Haven't tested it yet. I'll need root access."

"You're thinking we just query for those file names and not perform a more comprehensive assessment?"

"I expect the Germans will approve of my efficient approach."

"Well, call me Mr. Businessman, but I was thinking we'd accrue some billable hours here. Identify their requirements and hire some local consultants to perform a network security assessment. Could be the start of a European practice."

"We close our transaction with CBI in eight days, Rob. Why are you focused on growing the business? We're selling out dude."

"Hmm, yeah, I don't know. Habit. I've been doing this non-stop the last year. It's what I do."

"Well, time to stop. CBI doesn't even want to retain us after closing. Apparently, our previous HR records are tainted. In eight days, we'll both be retired. And wealthy."

Greg paused to consider Rob's true motive. "I know you, Rob. You want to solve this thing. Let's just do this job as quickly as we can and go home. I was talking with the Major before I boarded my flight. I'm the last guy to sow fear, but I'd like to get back home before the airlines suffer a major cyberattack."

"Calvert say that was going to happen?"

"He didn't give any specifics, but I know him, and he sounded ominous."

"Oh, that's just Calvert being Calvert. Here we go again, Cyber War II. He's probably being followed around by a press crew."

Greg laughed. "He probably is."

***

Later that Sunday night, Calvert was being interviewed live on German television by a highly attractive frau. He didn't know it, but Maria Pfeiffer was possibly the most well-known and respected journalist on the European continent, having made her latest splash documenting chemical weapons attacks in Syria with graphic video of suffering children. It was said one of her Syrian episodes was correlated with a spike in the sale of Kleenex facial tissues from millions of crying Germans. She smelled a story around Calvert, who spoke German with a level three fluency that made him appear adorable on camera, like a little boy.

"Major Calvert, thank you for making yourself available to speak to this story of a massive, distributed denial of service attack against the American banking system over the weekend. Can you walk us through what happened?"

"Absolutely, Frau Pfeiffer. If you can please excuse my broken Deutsch. I'm hoping that, with a little immersion over the next week, it'll come back to me."

"Oh, we understand you fine, Major Calvert. Please continue." Maria pictured in her mind her ratings soar as frauen throughout Germany kept their channel dialed-in to watch this sexy American military man talk with the sophistication of a third-grade schoolboy with his broken German.

"Well, to begin with, we haven't classified this attack as a DDoS - or as you say, distributed denial of service attack. Systems didn't crash, they didn't even slow down. I think what's happened is the story has emerged on how we leveraged DDoS mitigation methods to counter the attack. That was just some really clever thinking by the engineers at our American telecommunications firms, but we're classifying this attack as part of a hybrid warfare campaign launched by Russia. This is cyberwar."

Maria was stunned. Her network canceled the show she had planned for tonight to host this story instead, because they had this Calvert guy available to speak. He had a history of making a splash in the media. She watched some clips of him speaking on some cyberattack a year earlier as part of prepping for tonight's show.

He did appear to own that interview, and the event drove the news cycle for the subsequent two weeks. Her network director was almost yelling in her earpiece with his excitement. He instructed her to delve into the Russia connection.

"Are you saying Russia has launched a cyberattack against the United States of America? Does that require NATO to invoke Article 5's collective defense clause?"

"Well, not Article 5 exactly Frau Pfeiffer, but NATO has recently strengthened provisions to jointly counter cyberattacks. I hate to disappoint you, but I'm not at liberty to go into details of plans around acting on those provisions at this time. And frankly, there is very little precedence to act on those provisions."

Calvert's mission on this news show was in fact aimed at alerting Russia of his intentions to counterattack. To spin up their strategic planning resources and if nothing else, get them to lose a few hours of sleep. He intended to lead them on a misdirection campaign in Ukraine while the red team would hit them across the border from the Baltics. All this while also announcing surprise war games in the Baltics.

The only way to slow down Russia's cyber-aggression was to put them on defense. That was the essential goal of their plan, Operation Xs and Os. The more immediate goal was to aid Ukraine in a counterattack against Russian Separatists, making his initial foray into Ukraine a double reverse of sorts, sticking with the football metaphor. Countering whatever Russia was doing in the energy sector would be a bonus. Only problem was NATO hadn't yet figured out what that cyberattack was all about. The thought was that by pushing Russia to speed up their timetable, they might trip up and expose themselves on that front.

The interview played well for both Maria and Calvert. After the show, Calvert rode a late train to Halle, where he intended to speak to a cybersecurity class at Martin Luther University. An effort to allow Russia the chance to follow his transparent trek toward Ukraine. Fitzmaurice designed the concept, Calvert could claim credit for the project name which spoke to football player positions in a game plan.

***

General Alexander Volkov was on the phone with Putin, whose permission he needed to speed up the rate of their hybrid war exercises.

"Goddammit, Sasha! What is Calvert doing in Frankfurt? He should be home protecting his own country's financial center."

"It's not good, Mr. President." The two men were close personal friends, but the General was not at liberty to call Putin by his common name. "It can only indicate he is needed in Europe to lead something of significance."

"Why don't we know what that is?"

"What we do know sir is that American cyber recon has accelerated in recent months against Ukraine and Crimea. Their focus is on Ukraine."

"That's where our focus is, Sasha. That's not good."

"Understood, sir. But our more immediate focus is on the destabilization of the Western European green energy sector to increase the contract prices for Nord Stream 2. Ukraine is the long game. We'll accelerate our short game while the Americans are spending dollars in Ukraine."

"Make it happen, Sasha. You have my support. But no more fucking wet ops. That doesn't appear to be Fancy Bear's strength. Stick to cyber." Putin hung up the secure phone.

***

The local craft brew appeared to be putting Greg to sleep, so Rob talked him into joining him for a tour of the nearby Beatle's Museum. This didn't wake Greg up. They completed the tour a bit quicker than Rob would like because he could tell his younger partner didn't seem to appreciate it to the extent he did. They soon found themselves in the pub attached to their hotel reminiscing about their past year working with their assassinated partner, Justin.

"I was in the military, Rob. I sliced my hand open once adding a memory card to a computer. That's the most danger I was ever in. Justin didn't deserve this. He wasn't working for CyberCom, he was a bloody consultant."

"He was good too. And just over a week from becoming a multi-millionaire. Did you know he was back with his wife?"

"He told me things were looking good between them. Would she get anything with him dying before the sale? I'd be willing to give her part of my shares if not."

"You've got a big heart Greg, but yeah, they actually got married last week. I talked to Bill yesterday, and he said Justin completed paperwork to make Meagan his beneficiary even if they weren't married, so she'll be fine."

"Good to hear." Greg quaffed down the middle half of his pint. "So Rob, you're a smart guy. You were just thrown off a cliff by a Russian assassin. Very likely GRU related to the wind farm hack. Why are you doing this?"

Rob hadn't formulated his response to this yet but knew he should prepare for when Sue asked the same question.

"I haven't totally thought it through yet. You're right, I'm not looking for one more quick contract. Justin was killed over this. Don't you feel some sort of obligation to know why?"

"We will know why. Ultimately, the story will come out. I'm not afraid for myself Rob, but I do have a wife and baby at home. You said Sue is very likely coming out. My point is, this isn't just cybercrime. It's cyber-fucking-war. And it's the Russians."

"You're right. You can go home if you want Greg. I'm sorry for bringing you out here. That was selfish."

"I'm not going home. They killed Justin. I've been on a dozen assignments with him over the past year."

"Good, I'm going to need your tech skills with this energy firm tomorrow. Personally, I'm more worried about Calvert finding out I didn't return home. Your buddy scares me sometimes."

"He already knows. He doesn't mind it when he thinks you're working for him. Everyone's a contractor under his employ, in his worldview. He has a team tracking you for your protection. I think I spotted them back at the museum. Twenty-year-olds don't go to museums. One looks eerily like Calvert, ten years younger. That's what made me notice them."

"Calvert's a piece of work." Rob finished off his pint.

"He is. But they attacked his five-month pregnant wife. Fair to say the gloves are off. It's getting late, let me grab some menus."

Greg finished his pint while he sauntered up to the bar for a fourth round and menus. As the barmann drew the pints, Greg looked up to the flatscreen behind the bar to see Calvert being interviewed by an absolutely stunning journalist on Sky. Greg recognized the channel because his wife streamed it back home to watch The Affair. He didn't know Calvert could speak German. He felt the jet lag and pledged to go to bed immediately after dinner.

Chapter Eight

SITTING alone in his first-class cabin, on the train from Frankfurt to Halle, Calvert directed the NATO troops seconded to him via his secure phone.

"Captain, are you confident you can have all your troops back across the border before Monday morning. NATO announces war games for the NRF at 0900."

"Yessir. Minsk will be the furthest intrusion into Belarus. And no troops will need to enter dense urban areas. The radios they plant will be miles from their target emergency alert systems."

"And these men have left their smartphones at home, correct?"

"Yessir. These men do not have smartphones and have never maintained social media accounts."

"Run through the plan one more time for me please, Captain."

"Yessir. Twelve two-man teams have been entering into twelve Belarusian metro areas near the Lithuanian border throughout the day. The last team crossed ninety minutes ago. They'll reach their targets by 2400.

"After confirmation from you to me at 2400, they'll place radio transmitters in hidden locations in wooded areas near the towns. The troops will then begin their return to Lithuania, targeting completion by 0300, well before the announcement of the NATO Response Force war games.

"The radios will begin transmitting the tonal commands to activate their respective sirens at 0300 Tuesday. The tonal commands will play for ten minutes, repeating at random intervals for two hours. The radios will then self-detonate."

"Very good, Captain. There is no reason to take any risks here that would result in casualties. Make sure your men are aware to proceed with extreme caution. If we can get just half these radios into play, we'll achieve mission success."

"Understood, Major."

Calvert hung up. As if his military khakis weren't enough, his secure phone was noticeably bigger than typical smartphones and two different men had walked by his glass-walled cabin since he'd been talking, stealing glances. He was confident his communications couldn't be decrypted, quite possibly for the next decade, but one never knew if certain techniques might not determine who he'd been communicating with. He put the phone away, set his watch for 11:45 and closed his eyes for some long-overdue sleep.

His Xs & Os operation was part of the larger NATO NRF war games exercise, code-named Operation NeRF Ball, for NATO electronic Response Forces War Games. Ball denoted war games. The "e" for electronic, represented participation by Cyber Ops to demonstrate NATO's hybrid warfare capabilities. As such, it was intended to be somewhat obvious rather than stealthy. If all went well, Calvert's involvement would be limited. If things escalated, due to the unexpected disruption of an apparent Russian cyberattack on the European energy industry, Calvert might not sleep again for a very long time.

***

"These two files are indeed suspicious, having the same names as the two malicious files we found last week. One of them is larger though. I suspect it contains more functionality, possibly calling home to a C2 server."

"C2?" The systems engineer asked Greg to explain the term.

"Stands for Command and Control. I used to always say CnC but the industry lately has come to use the term C2. Infected systems will communicate with a C2 server, termed calling home, like from the 1980s movie E.T." Greg expected some recognition from the twenty-eight-year-old engineer but didn't get any.

"The C2 server can collect data, or give the infected system new instructions to carry out further attacks. It can even update the malware to perform spam campaigns one day, and a DDoS attack the next. A single C2 server can control thousands of bots, but there are oftentimes multiple C2s to maintain control as you block access at your firewall. Can you give me permission to transfer your firewall logs back to Austin? My staff there have the tools to search for C2s these two files might be communicating with."

Greg and Rob were standing in a conference room of a large energy firm with the systems engineer, Stephan Franke, who engaged them, the company CISO, or Chief Information Security Officer, Max Freitag, who signed them a check for twenty-five thousand dollars, and a woman who processed the paperwork for Max. There were chairs, but for some reason the Germans preferred standing, so Greg and Rob stood as well.

Greg projected his laptop screen on the wall so everyone could watch him query the image file of a server that Stephan expected was compromised. He searched for the file names of the malware found in the U.K. breach and quickly discovered them. That they were also encrypted and one contained the same number of bytes suggested that they are similar malware.

Max responded, "Absolutely. Please engage the full force of your team back home."

Greg began uploading the firewall logs to his secure DropBox site. He could parse through the logs himself, and eventually would. His true intent was to share the logs with Sara for her work with Calvert. He'd email a link to Sara after the upload completed.

"Stephan, I just emailed you a routine that will crawl through your network and record all the hostnames where it finds these two files. It'll prompt you for admin credentials that will give it access to each server. Nothing else for us to do now, we can meet back tomorrow morning with our findings from your firewall logs. Same time?" Greg looked at Rob as he said this, knowing he should let him take over the conversation.

Max responded, "Yes, 9 am. Joyce will meet you in the lobby and escort you back here."

Rob was not quite yet ready to leave. He was interested in learning more on the industry.

"Max, I'm somewhat familiar with the oil and gas industry. They suffer from about three hundred terrorist attacks a year. Many of them are cyberattacks. I'm afraid I know very little though about green energy. I wouldn't guess you as a target of hacktivists - hackers out to harm your business for social or political causes?"

"Correct, we don't see much activity from known hacktivists. We get our share of recon from Lazarus and Fancy Bear - nation states. We've never detected a breach. We run a DLP platform to ensure no data leaves our premises network without authorization, and monitor brand protection. Again, most of our findings point to Fancy Bear. Never anything serious. We require two-factor authentication for all remote access. We run a tight ship."

"Yeah, well two-factor is brilliant. Not enough firms run data loss protection either, so good for you. Interesting most of your hits point to Fancy Bear."

"Indeed. Lazarus is a distant second."

"Tell me about your firm. Are you a large operator?"

"One of the largest in Germany. We operate three thousand towers. Mostly in and around here in the state of Saxony. Germany's Energiewende policy has been promoting offshore, higher yield, but we've yet to expand there."

"Is it a seasonal business. When the wind blows?" Rob attempted humor but Max missed it in translation.

"Production is less constant onshore but Energiewende guarantees us a fixed income. We've nearly completed the shut down of all nuclear plants in Germany. It's a strong market with government backing like that."

"I see." Rob mirrored Max's serious face. "And you say this breach is already crimping your energy production? Can you tell me by how much?"

"No, sorry Rob, I'm not at liberty to say in nominal terms. I can say we have ten percent of our towers under repair or shut down waiting for repair. That's high. Your check for twenty-five thousand euros is a drop in the bucket."

"Oh, was it euros?" Rob thought to himself that he just made another five thousand dollars by not being clear his quote was in dollars.

***

Rob found himself back at the Leipzig-Halle airport after his profitable meeting with the wind farm operator. Greg stayed back at the hotel to parse through firewall logs. Sue found a later flight than what Greg came in on, but it will still arrive at a good time to eat lunch at the same little airport sandwich shop Rob discovered yesterday. He texted Sue with instructions for her to meet him there. She walked up to find him sipping a beer.

"A little early to be drinking isn't it darling?"

Rob looked up. "Sue. Airports exist between time zones, free from all temporal conventions. And this is Germany. How was your flight?"

"Fine, but I have to say, it feels odd to find myself here after just speaking to you on the phone, barely twenty-four hours ago, from home." She seated herself.

"You look okay. I was expecting bandages or something."

"A few scrapes on my hands." He held them up for her to inspect. "I have a bruise on my chin, but I've yet to shave."

"I've noticed. I can put some blush on that once you do."

"To see more, you'll have to wait for me to take off my shirt back at the Dormero Hotel Halle."

"Sounds romantic."

"There's a shop near the hotel that sells authentic German dirndls."

"I didn't fly halfway around the world to play dress-up for you, mister."

"Halfway would have landed you in China. How's our little girl?"

"Oh Rob, not good. The OBGYN said it's not a viable pregnancy. She told Ella that the heart stopped beating after seven weeks gestation. She'll go back in next week and take a pill if she doesn't spontaneously miscarry first."

"Oh no. That's horrible. Why did you fly here, Sue? You should have stayed with Ella."

"She has to go through this with Ethan. They're common-law married now, and they need to experience this together. He attended the doctor visit with her."

"That's good. She get on his insurance?"

"Yes. That's why they made the common law official."

"That's right, I forgot. Not because they love each other."

"Rob, stop. I think they do. They get through this and they'll be strong. Ella's still planning on a wedding next summer. She's looking at the Little Nell in Aspen."

"Holy Christ. We can't afford that, Sue."

"I think maybe we can."

Rob often forgot that he was about to become a multi-millionaire.

"Hmm. I feel so bad for her. We really were lucky, weren't we?"

"Yes, we were."

"I like letting Blake know he was an accident, then telling Ella she was planned."

"You're the only one who finds that funny, Rob."

"Ella gonna be okay?"

"She'll be okay."

"So, seriously, with all that, why'd you fly out here?"

"Because I know what you're up to, Rob. You're going to keep working this cyberattack to make up for Justin's death. You weren't going to come home. I had to pick between husband and daughter to care for, and Ella has Ethan. I'm not going to sit at home in a state of worry, harping on you to return. Best course of action is to join you where I can be in command and control. We have to be back home for Ella's next OBGYN visit on Monday."

Rob found Sue's logic compelling. And it occurred to him that she'd spared him from having to explain himself, which he couldn't.

He wasn't sure if he should be happy or sad just now. First, he got pushed over a cliff. That led to a new gig where he scored an additional five thousand dollars on his consulting agreement from a currency misunderstanding. Then the news on Ella's pregnancy.

Still, he was in Germany sipping a beer, and his wife obviously loved him. He pictured Sue wearing a drindl back at the hotel. It would do them both some good.

"You're in charge, Sue."

***

Greg joined Rob and Sue for dinner at the Taparazzi, a short walk from their hotel. They spent the afternoon walking around the town center and worked up an appetite. Sue was captivated by the quaintness of the traditional German dress shop and, feeling in a vacation mood, bought the drindl to wear for Rob later. She ordered a French Chardonnay while the boys drank the Warsteiner pilsner that was served on tap. Turned out the restaurant was aptly named as the menu consisted mostly of tapas. They ordered a healthy round of half the items.

Rob couldn't help but talk a little business.

"You parse logs all day, Greg?"

"You know parsing's my passion, Rob."

Rob chuckled. Greg could say something was his passion in almost any discussion. It was his go-to line.

"I did find seven C2s. A new one each day, then the pattern repeats, cycling through the same seven sites each week."

"Wow, you really have been working."

"Not really. I uploaded the logs to ThreatConnect. I went for a run, showered. Walked around the town center. Saw those two twenty-year-olds standing outside a dress shop. Came back and read my report on the seven C2s. Let's tell the client though that our team in Austin worked through the night."

"Sounds like a plan."

They clinked their pilsners.

"What two twenty-year-olds?"

Rob knew that wouldn't escape Sue.

"Our protection, darling. Courtesy of the U.S. Military. Just Calvert being cautious. Nothing to worry about."

Sue understood and felt almost spoiled by the thought of active duty servicemen watching over her. The conversation turned to things to do in Germany as a tourist.

***

Putin rarely expressed his anger through words, but Alexander knew him well enough to read his tone.

"Sasha, as I assume you are aware, NATO announced war games for their rapid response force in the Baltics. I have two questions for you. Despite their pretense of this being a last minute decision, why did we not already know about these plans? And two, I was awoken last night to receive reports of emergency response sirens randomly playing throughout the night. Explain that to me please."

"Mr. President, we did report on the increase in communications between U.S. Cybercom and NATO forces beginning in the spring. We didn't know why, but this now explains it. And the hack into local emergency response systems illustrates their plan to include a degree of hybrid warfare in their exercises."

"Please tell me, Sasha, how they did that."

The overuse of the word please is how Alexander knew the president was upset.

"Most likely radio frequencies, Mr. President. Those systems are not connected to the Internet. A similar attack against the city of Dallas, Texas was carried out earlier this year. Possibly CyberCom practicing."

"Are you suggesting this is not practice now?"

"I believe it's part of their exercises. I have my men searching near the towns now in Belarus for the radios. If they launch their strike again tonight, we'll be prepared to triangulate their sources."

"You mean NATO actually crossed the border for this attack?"

Putin expressed surprise.

"The borders of Belarus, yes Mr. President. The nature of the sirens' RF power suggests the transmitters need to be within twenty or so kilometers of their targets. This gives us a good chance to catch them, Mr. President."

"Good, Sasha. If you capture prisoners, try not to kill any of them. I don't like how this is escalating at such a critical time for our wind farm operation. I'm considering a delay for our operation to take the Baltics. I have to assume this surprise war games exercise is NATO's way of telling us they know something. What are your thoughts on that?"

"We need to monitor for anything they leave in place after their exercises, Mr. President. This shouldn't impact our timing unless they deploy some tech that could counter our attack. Our energy operation is more fragile now though sir, with the recent U.K. discovery. My plans are to accelerate the timeline.

"I've ordered an increase in the frequency of mechanical interference with the onshore wind farm operation. We don't have C2 communication with offshore systems, but I expect a meaningful drop in total European energy output this month - in time for the summer heat of August. And I've accelerated the disinformation campaign on social networks. Should I continue with those operations, sir?"

"Sasha, you haven't changed from when we were kids. Always the first to strike, Fancy Bear. Our economy can still benefit from this. Nord Stream 2 is a year out from completion. Our customers are signing energy contracts now. Continue your efforts to sabotage their energy infrastructure, even if our military objectives are put on hold. Good work, Sasha. Let's keep these daily briefings throughout the NATO exercises."

Putin ended the call.

Alexander understood the role his cyberwar efforts played as part of his country's economic goals, but he couldn't steer his thoughts away from the energies futures he purchased. Not just him, nearly every oligarch he knew had personal skin in this game. Altogether, they stood to either make or lose hundreds of millions. For his well-being, it had better be the former.

***

Sara never drank coffee before coming to the Doughnut, but she does now. She hadn't felt comfortable staying alone in the B&B

that Major Calvert put her up in. Everyone there was so old. She began sleeping on a cot in a room with a couple of other female contractors at the Doughnut Sunday night. She quickly mimicked the other girls' 18-hour work schedules, and coffee was just part of the routine.

She carried her cold cup of joe up to the podium in the hundred seat auditorium where she was requested just five minutes prior to provide a briefing on her findings to date. The room was half full of mostly men in uniform. She sipped her coffee as a private plugged her off-net laptop into the video adapter that would project her monitor onto a wall-sized screen behind her.

Sara found that she wasn't nervous. Her advanced classes at school prepared her well for this. She briefed Calvert on a secure video chat the previous night, and he instructed her to make some PowerPoint charts. She was glad she stayed up late last night doing that so she had something for this morning's surprise briefing. Even though she only had a single slide, she hoped people would appreciate the graphic of a wind tower she added alongside the bullets.

"Well hello. My name is Sara Thomas. I'm sorry, I don't know how to address all of you, and I'm not entirely sure what you want to see. I'll just start by showing you a slide that summarizes my findings over the last two or three days. Please feel free to ask questions.

"My objective was to analyze server logs from as many wind towers as possible. From wind farms, I should say, that are located within Europe. I've obtained close to thirty thousand logs from ten thousand servers. That's less than one hundred percent of all towers deployed within Europe, but it's orders of magnitude more than what's needed to form a viable statistical sample.

"My logs are all from Saturday, Sunday and Monday. The hope was to obtain logs before they were modified. The first thing I can infer from these logs, based on their timestamps, is that the malware cron job that modifies them runs every hour. That keeps the useful data short."

Sara said this last statement as a joke, which she realized was for her benefit only since no one laughed.

"Finding number two is that the anomalous log readings are evident in over ninety-nine percent of the server logs. Because, from my last statement, only the final hour of logs from three days are unmodified.

"Finding number three comes from the server images, where we found the exact same two malware files as were discovered initially in the U.K. I say *exact* when referring to the name but finding number four is that for one of the files, it's size is larger for onshore wind towers than offshore, suggesting additional functionality.

"I can infer what this functionality is with finding number five, which came this time from a small set of firewall logs I obtained from a German energy firm with only onshore towers. They all communicate with a rotating set of seven C2s. I could then infer that other logs found to be communicating with those C2s were also from onshore wind farms."

It didn't occur to Sara to define C2s as command and control servers for her audience. She assumed them all to be smarter than herself. The first voice shouted out from the audience, asked this question. She responded and made a mental note that perhaps not everyone was smarter than her.

"The only other firewall logs I have are from the initial breach here from offshore towers in the U.K. They don't show communication with a C2, supporting my earlier inference. We'll know for sure once we've decrypted those files. I've requested firewall logs going forward. They really help to add context to the server logs.

"Finding number six is what I believe to be the source of the C2s. They are rented from the Alpha Bay Market dark web marketplace. This site is run by twenty-year-old Andrei Popov, out of Macedonia. He's known to work for the GRU, making him part of Fancy Bear's operation. I can't say that he's behind it. More likely it's one of his marketplace clients. But he's a real person with a name."

Once the audience could see that Sara was out of bullets, the questions flooded in.

"Can we assume there's an ownership connection between the malware and the C2 sites?"

"Unfortunately, no ma'am. The malware could be rented out separately and paired with the botnet that's controlled by the C2s."

"You seem to be suggesting though that this Popov guy is a person of interest?"

"Yes, sir. He might not know anything about the malware or the botnet they are running on and the C2s, but his customers make up a community. And he is a known associate of Fancy Bear, based on the profile database maintained off-net here at the Doughnut. I'm speculating now, but what I hear around the water cooler is that Russia is a prime suspect. Honestly, it's pretty rare to have a name to start with so quickly on these investigations. Even if he doesn't know about it, he's linked to it via his marketplace. So he's a starting place, if nothing else."

The questions continued for the next half hour, but were mostly answered by others in the room. As soon as she was excused, she headed to the bathroom to relieve herself from the effects of the morning's caffeine.

***

"Guten tag, Max. Good to see you again. Joyce treated us to these coffees on our way up. Very much appreciated."

"I look forward to approving the expense report. Just kidding. Thank you, Joyce, for escorting these gentlemen in this morning. Any new information, Rob?"

"I'm going to let Greg take you through his findings. I do think we have everything we need, and we will provide you with a more detailed report next week after our team has spent more time reviewing your logs."

Rob and Greg were presenting in the same conference room where they met with Max, Stephan, and Joyce yesterday. Stephan was seated at the long table already and joined by four other men. Rob assumed them to be part of Max's information security organization. Max didn't introduce them, and Rob couldn't gain a sense of how technical any of them were. It didn't help that the room was darker than Rob would prefer, lighted by only the sunlight through the blinds. Rob didn't know if the German penchant for keeping the lights off was to save money or energy, or if somehow they were still trying to avoid presenting themselves as a bombing target. He kept those thoughts to himself as Greg powered up his laptop and one of the others connected it to the projector.

The room settled down with everyone in seats, something Rob noted as different from the previous day when they remained standing. Greg began his presentation.

"I said I would research possible communication with C2 servers so I'll start there."

Max demonstrated early that this would be a dialog by asking, "You researched more than the firewall logs?"

"Not exactly, no. I do have some related news to share with you though. We'll get to it, this will be a fairly short briefing.

"My team did indeed determine that the malware we discovered is communicating with seven known command and control servers. I say known because we actually know quite a bit about them."

Greg stretched the truth here because while he did discover the seven C2 servers himself from his ThreatConnect query, Sara's military information was the source of his deeper findings on the Alpha Bay owner profile.

"These C2s are rented out by a dark web marketplace named Alpha Bay Market. The marketplace itself is run by a well-known hacker with close ties to Fancy Bear, named Andrei Popov. He resides in Macedonia, where he's protected by local officials, namely his father who is the chief of police for the town he resides in, and ultimately, Russia."

One of the other men, who had yet to be introduced, spoke up. He was young, possibly in his twenties still, with strikingly white blonde hair slicked back into a short ponytail.

"Are you suggesting we've been attacked by Fancy Bear? By Russia?"

"Well, clearly I haven't had enough time to substantiate that. But hacktivists don't pay to use the tools at this marketplace. And the Russian connection is hard to ignore."

"Fair enough."

"Good. So the only other meaningful data point is the pattern of the malware communicating with seven C2s, a new one each day. And then repeating that pattern each week to the same servers. That might not sound super clever, but it does point to a more expensive C2 rental than the average malware attack that would only use one or two C2s."

"The same blonde asked, "So you're suggesting we're up against someone with some resources behind them?"

"Exactly. This is an advanced, persistent attack. This is professional. Still, it's only seven C2s. We know their IPs, and you can block them now at your firewalls."

Max responded. "Good suggestion. I see you're out of slides, but you said there was another topic to discuss. Something related?"

"Yes, I did." Greg looked to Rob to take over.

Rob cleared his throat.

"Max, conventionally, the next step for you would be to bring in an incident response team to help you navigate through the requisite forensics. You'll need to fully understand the scope of this breach before you communicate anything to authorities."

"I would argue the next step would be to update my resume Rob, but yes, I was going to begin asking you questions on incident response."

"I'm glad to see you have a sense of humor, Max. I'm not sure how you'll react to what I have to share with you next. The good news is that incident response won't cost your company a single euro."

Rob paused, but Max remained quiet. Patient for the other shoe to drop.

"The bad news, depending on how you look at it, is that a cyber response team from NATO will be showing up this afternoon to take over the investigation."

Rob didn't have to pause this time before Max responded.

"I'm not overly surprised, Rob. I saw you on television last year at the Vegas casino with a Captain Calvert running the show. So I understand that you seem to have some connections with the military."

"He's Major Calvert now. He did well from that."

Rob hoped Max still had his sense of humor.

He did, as evidenced by a chuckle.

"No worries, Rob. I'll be able to spin the money this will save my firm. Let's hope it protects my position too as a matter of national security."

Max's light-hearted and confident nature put Rob at ease. It was clear to Rob this guy had experience and was confident he could work anywhere else if he lost this job. They ended the meeting with Rob promising Max to keep him apprised of developments beyond the scope of their engagement. They were in this together.

***

Rob and Greg returned to their separate hotel rooms after the meeting. Greg caught up on some work. Rob hung out in the room planning lunch with Sue. The three of them walked together just after noon, two kilometers across the urban center, to what they expected to be a modern German restaurant. Sue noted it was rated five of five on TripAdvisor.

As Greg opened the door for Sue and Rob, a young man shuffled in as well, apparently running up behind them.

"Thank you, sir."

Greg recognized the young man, well-dressed in pressed blue jeans, button-down and sports jacket, as one of the two men whom he guessed had been keeping an eye on them recently for their safety.

"I feel like I should know you."

"Private Yankee, sir. I expect you've noticed me following you around recently?" The man spoke with a British accent.

Sue and Rob were standing behind the gentleman, and Sue was the first to respond.

"Oh, you must be our protection?"

"Yes, ma'am."

Rob, somewhat incredulous, asked, "Is Yankee seriously your last name?"

"Yes, sir. It's a real name. I'm British, sir. I'll be joining the three of you for lunch until Major Calvert can take my seat. He's running a few minutes late."

Rob and Greg looked at each other and Sue responded, "It'll be our pleasure to dine with you, private."

"Thank you, ma'am."

The host sat them outside on the sidewalk with flowering, hanging baskets and a view of the many office workers walking to and from lunch. Private Yankee explained that Major Calvert was in town to present a speech on cybersecurity at Martin Luther University. The speech was in the morning and he was running a few minutes behind because he was walking. The major arrived before the waiter took their food order, and the private excused himself.

Greg greeted Calvert first. "Running behind schedule today, Major?"

"You picked a restaurant on the far side from where I was walking. Anything close to the hotel or in another direction and I'd have been on time, if not early. It's really your fault that I'm late. Who hikes two kilometers to lunch?"

"I picked the restaurant Major," replied Sue. "I don't think we've been introduced."

Calvert extended his hand to shake. "Indeed, we haven't met,

Mrs. Warner. I'm Major James Calvert. I've had the pleasure of working alongside your fine husband for the past year. It's very nice to finally meet you."

Calvert seated himself and smiled broadly at Greg and Rob. Greg almost expected this. Rob was speechless.

"Mr. Warner, I think the last time we spoke, Friday was it, you indicated you'd be heading home?"

"Needs of the business, Major. We have a new client here in Halle. Sue decided to join me, and we're making somewhat of a vacation out of it."

"That must be nice. Is your business finished then?"

"I believe it is, Major. Sue and I were coming up with ideas on places to visit for the rest of the week. We fly home Sunday."

Rob could never figure Calvert out. He knew that Calvert knew his business was finished. NATO took over the incident response.

"That's good to hear. I should tell you, little Sara is doing an awesome job for us at the Doughnut. I appreciate you being so flexible with her internship commitments. She not only made short work out of analyzing logs from literally tens of thousands of servers, but she presented a report this morning identifying a six-month social media campaign by Fancy Bear, steering public opinion against renewable energy. Has she shared that with you?"

"I just read that an hour ago. I thought we'd talk about that over lunch."

Greg jumped in. "I read it this morning too. Clearly, this is a continuation of Russia taking Crimea and battling with Ukraine. Last month's Notpetya attack was just another cyberattack in a long-term campaign. This is their long-term plan for dominance in the European energy market."

"My thoughts exactly, Greg" confirmed the Major. "And I can tell you, there won't be another Crimea. We're going to put a stop to this."

Rob, Greg, and Sue all felt a bit of excitement with the Major's statement. He was wearing his dress uniform and his words imbued a sense of pending action. The waiter arrived to take their order, prolonging their anticipation to learn more details. Calvert continued after the waiter left.

"That's all I can say on that topic. It's public news of course that NATO is currently conducting war games in the Baltic States. I've been maintaining high visibility the last few days, appearing on major media and presenting this morning at the university here in Halle."

Calvert paused to butter his bread and take a bite.

"Man, this butter is good."

Sue responded, "There's salt sprinkled on it, local from the area."

"Mmm. Now, without going into detail, I need to become invisible for a couple of days. And I could use your help with that."

"You need *our* help?" Rob asked this purposefully sounding incredulous.

"I do. It feels good working together again, doesn't it?" Calvert asked this both facetiously and rhetorically, so Rob didn't bother to answer.

"Private Yankee's partner, Private Triolo, whom you haven't met, but maybe you've seen walking around, is nearly my twin brother. I'm going to stealthily leave my hotel room later this afternoon to rent a car, and I won't be returning. As part of operation doppelgänger, Private Triolo will join you for dinner tonight, and then breakfast tomorrow. All I ask is that you greet him with my name. Loud enough for other tables to hear. In exchange for your brave patriotism, Private Triolo will pick up the tab for your meals."

"Deal." Rob said this a little too quickly, exposing his frugalness. Calvert learned something new about Rob from this, Greg wasn't surprised, and Sue felt somewhat embarrassed. Rob sensed all this and felt slighted as his actual glee was from knowing Calvert was leaving so soon. He determined to let it go as clarification wouldn't help his cause. He turned the conversation back on the topic of Sara.

"I was going to respond earlier Major, that I should be thanking you for the opportunity you've provided Sara. With working at the Doughnut on her resume, she'll have her pick of universities, if not scholarships, anywhere in the country."

"Oh, little Sara can't put that on her resume. This is all fairly sensitive, Mr. Warner. She's been made aware of this. Besides, she'll be attending the Air Force Academy in Colorado Springs. Her work for me will be referenced in the letter of recommendation they'll receive."

Greg joined in, "The Academy is hardly a school of science, Major."

"Au contraire. And after the excitement that girl will have

experienced this week, she'll only be thinking of serving her country. Nothing compares."

Rob figured it out. "You sent her to the U.K. just to recruit her?"

"ROTC doesn't exactly produce computer scientists, Mr. Warner. There's a war for talent if you haven't noticed. I'm always recruiting. Always."

The conversation sparred back and forth through lunch, competitively debating everything from the best food town, Austin won, to the merits of fly fishing over hiking, because good fly fishing included hiking.

Calvert left the table early as he had a long drive ahead of him. After his departure, Rob and Greg shared their travel plans with Sue, detailing how the needs of the business required them to take a train through Eastern Europe. The passage should be beautiful, traveling through Prague, Bratislava, Budapest, and the mountains of Serbia, on their journey to Macedonia. They planned to leave after breakfast tomorrow.

Chapter Nine

DANICA heard the general shouting from the cell phone pressed against Andrei's ear.

"Our tactics have changed Andrei. Get started!"

"Yes, General." Andrei looked solemnly toward Danica as he pocketed his mobile.

"Poor baby, that didn't sound good. Come back to bed, darling."

"No, I have to go into the office. You should call your sister, see if she wants to have lunch in my place. I'm going to have to work early today."

"Oh, I'm sorry darling. I'll bring you back some Lake Trout Wontons. If I don't eat them all." Danica winked. "Why so glum, Andrei? I know before lunch is early but you do usually work on Tuesdays."

"That was Fancy Bear. Goddamned, cheap-ass Russians. I have to replace my command and control servers with scores of others that I'll have to actually pay for. And then rent the malware to launch a new campaign. And increase my spending on the social campaign. The general said he can't cover any of my charges.

"I can see how this is trending. A cyberstorm is coming and I feel a strong need to cover my assets. I should be profiting from cyberwar, not subsidizing it."

"Oh, poor baby. Come here."

Danica pulled back the covers to make room for Andrei to slip in beside her for a few minutes of cuddling before she showered for lunch.

***

Andrei's office was his lakeside house that he didn't live in. He employed four server admins, two with actual skills, the other two just school kids learning the tech. At least one person was always working in the house day and night, ostensibly to keep the systems running, as an early warning system, should anyone come looking for him.

He knocked on his own door because that was the procedure. Paul, his most skilled tech but broader in girth than the width of the doorway, let him in. Paul was surprised to see Andrei breathing heavy in running gear.

"You run over here from the hotel? That's a good five kilometers."

"Yeah. My little brother challenged me to swim in the Ohrid Swimming Marathon this summer. That's twenty-nine kilometers in Lake Ohrid. I need to drop a few pounds."

"Hmm." Weighing twice as much as Andrei, Paul couldn't relate. "This is early for you. Something up, boss?"

"Yep. I got to reconfigure my C2s supporting the wind campaign. You been monitoring spot prices for C2s? They can't be from our site."

"Not today no, but prices are generally low this time of year. Nothing big going on."

"Good. Run a query and let me know the cheapest marketplace. I'm going to need about two dozen. Look at weekly rates. I got to take a shower."

After his shower, Andrei walked into the server room in shorts and a light blue tee that matched his eyes. He converted this room from his garage, the only room in the house without windows. He found the printout of C2 rates laying on his keyboard and scanned it.

The rates were reasonable and wouldn't cost him nearly as much as upping the intensity of the social media campaign with bots targeting Twitter and Facebook. He shouldn't have worried. He should be able to maintain his expenses under ten thousand U.S. dollars for this campaign if he could keep the duration under a month.

He instructed Paul on what to do and sat outside on his deck overlooking the lakeside restaurant where his girlfriend was eating lunch with her sister. Running a malware campaign was exhausting.

He heard the sliding glass door behind him open and close, and turned expecting to see Paul asking for additional instructions. Instead he saw Major Calvert, dressed not unlike his high school server admins, in cargo shorts and a black teeshirt with a 2016 DefCon logo. The mature loafers suggested Calvert was not a kid though. And after a second, Andrei recognized Calvert. Everyone in his industry had watched YouTube videos of Calvert orchestrating a cyberwar counterattack from a Vegas casino. Calvert was famous in Andrei's world, and he'd been communicating with him regularly over email for the last year.

"Paul let you in?"

"Is that his name?"

Increasingly alarmed, "Is Paul okay?"

"Paul will be fine, Andrei. We need to talk. Mind if I sit down?"

***

Sue could complain about a number of things on the Wednesday train ride through Eastern Europe. While clean, the train accommodations were far from luxurious. But the romance of the experience was undeniable.

The countryside looked nothing like the States, with countless, small villages, each with a church that looked older than America, fields of crops that weren't so much farms as they were cultivated plots. The large urban train stations, sometimes modern, others art deco, led her imagination into Agatha Christie stories. In their six by eight, first-class suite, overnight, they made love to the rhythmic passage.

Sue didn't preoccupy herself with Rob and Greg's plans until the morning after, an hour before they were to arrive at their destination in the quaint lakeside village of Ohrid, Macedonia. She entered the breakfast car well after Rob and Greg. She ordered fresh coffee, planning to nibble on Rob's leftover omelette and toast.

"I really enjoyed yesterday, just sitting and reading and looking out at the countryside. This really has turned into a vacation of sorts."

"Me too, sweetie. I'm glad you're enjoying it."

Greg felt differently. "This train could benefit from wifi. I've tethered my laptop to my mobile for Internet, but it's been spotty at best."

"Oh, being disconnected has been wonderful. What have you

boys been talking about this morning? Do we know what we're doing in Ohrid?"

They both returned sheepish looks. Greg started, knowing he would need to present the plan as much as possible, sounding like simply an extension of Sue's vacation.

"Sara has provided us with some impressive intel on the team behind the breach against the wind farms, which she was able to glean from the military systems. We don't know anything of course about the Russians who attacked Rob and Justin, and K.C., I almost forgot to add.

"But they're not our concern. All we can do is identify the actual hackers, who might be just paid pawns in the overall scheme of things. And if we can shut them down, that'll be enough. That will serve as retribution for Justin."

Sue looked to Rob. "Is that what this is about? Is that what you want, Rob? Retribution?"

Rob replied pensively, "I don't think that's it. Maybe a sense of closure?"

"This is how you define closure? Counterattacking their computers?"

Rob understood that Sue wasn't being mean. She was trying to help him understand himself, but coming up with responses was exasperating.

"I don't know, Sue. I'm probably not using the right words. It's not about revenge. I don't think so. I can't allow Justin's death to be the last word. To go unanswered, even though there aren't any answers. I want this Andrei guy to know who I am, and that I know who he is. I want him to know I did something about it."

"I see. Spoken like a guy, but I can understand how you feel, Rob. Let's move beyond the why and discuss the how. Since apparently introductions can't be accomplished by mailing a postcard, just what is our plan once we reach Ohrid?"

Rob looked to Greg to respond.

"Well, um, well, we figure we're going to need some sort of proximity attack. Meaning we'll need physical proximity to either breach his systems or perform a denial of service attack."

"I take it he lives in Ohrid?"

"Exactly. We have both his living and work addresses. Turns out, he lives in a hotel and works out of his house. We'll be staying in the same hotel. Sara gave us his coordinates, and we'll be staying in rooms along both sides of his. Yours is actually the best room in the hotel, Sue. With a separate bedroom and two baths."

"We could entertain." Some of Sue's facetiousness was so dry, it was only intended for herself.

Greg missed it.

"You totally could."

Rob understood he needed to further explain the plan to Sue.

"This is the plan, darling. Greg has a number of tools that work via Bluetooth. If Andrei has something enabled to listen to Bluetooth, he's got some good tech and can probably breach it. That'll be our beachhead into the Alpha Bay Marketplace."

"What will you be doing?" Sue picked up Rob's fork and helped herself to his leftovers.

"Us darling. What will we be doing? You and I will be conducting far more dangerous activities. Nothing cyber about it. We'll be in the field."

"The field?"

"We know what he looks like, and his girlfriend, but he doesn't know us. We'll be trying to sit next to him if he dines in the restaurant, or any place local. Living in a hotel, I have to assume he dines out."

"Are you going to talk to him?" Sue grabbed another bite.

"Talk? No. But as summer tourists, we'll be taking selfies. We'll take photo bombs of him so we can crop ourselves out later. We'll use these photos when we do begin to talk to him online."

"You're going to send him threatening emails?" Sue asked this before taking another forkful of eggs.

"Maybe. Not sure. I just know collecting the photos now will position us for some strong communication later. Might never use them."

"I see. It's not clear to me how this will make you boys feel better, but count me in, darling. Can I take your plate?"

***

By 4:40 pm, Rob and Sue were ensconced on a comfortable couch in the hotel lobby while Greg was in his room conducting operations. He'd already breached the phone of Andrei's girlfriend, whom he now knew to be Danica Ivanova.

Sue, much more visual than Rob, spotted Andrei as he entered the lobby. Andrei walked directly to the front desk, so Sue sprinted up behind him to overhear. Rob caught himself from falling asleep and recovered to ping Greg that Andrei was on his way up.

"Simon, please reserve that little lake view table in the рибар for seven will you?"

"Absolutely, no problem sir."

"Thanks."

Andrei turned for his room and excused himself in Macedonian as he passed by Sue, who nodded, not understanding the language.

Sue then talked to the man, Simon apparently, at the front desk.

"Excuse me, I think I heard that gentleman mention ribar. Is that how you pronounce the name of your restaurant?"

"Yes ma'am, it is. Ree-bar. He was just making a reservation for 7:00. Reservations aren't necessary if that's what you want. He just likes a special table by the window."

"Oh, well, if it's okay, my husband and I would like a nice table by the window too. For 6:45. Would you have something available?"

"Yes, ma'am. Absolutely, no problem. Mrs. Warner in room 505, correct?"

"Yes, thank you so much."

Sue returned to Rob on the sofa, who was somewhat stunned by her aggressiveness. He was awake now.

"What were you doing?"

"Field operations, Rob. We'll be dining in the hotel restaurant at a romantic window-side table, fifteen minutes before Andrei and his girlfriend sit next to us."

"You include Greg in our reservations?"

"Oh, I forgot about him. Can't he go somewhere else?"

"I guess he'll have to. What time is dinner then?"

"6:45. I'm going to head up to the room to get ready."

As he watched Sue walk to the elevator, Rob considered having another drink, with dinner still two full hours away. It occurred to him that Sue must be planning to dress up if she's taking two full hours to shower and dress. He could wear his dress shoes and one of his button-down work shirts, but would stick with blue jeans. The restaurant here looked nice, but he was on vacation. He waved a hand at the woman tending bar to indicate another draft.

***

With the restaurant half full, Rob and Sue were seated at the only two-top by the window. Sue was colorful, in a blue and yellow, flower-patterned maxi-dress and silver jewelry. Rob was comfortable in jeans and a white dress shirt. Reading the menu, he began the dialog, almost forgetting why they were there.

"These prices are nice. We could afford to retire here."

Sue responded. "It smells wonderful. Are you looking at the fish?"

"Let's start with caviar."

"And Prosecco?"

"Why not?"

Rob placed their order for starters with the waiter. Alone again, Sue turned to the topic of field operations.

"I would have expected Andrei to want this two top for him and his girlfriend. The other window table seats four."

"Maybe it has a better view?"

"Our tables look out the same window."

"Hmm. Would you pass the butter please, darling?"

After finishing their starter and placing their dinner order, Sue, facing the empty table, was the first to see Andrei and Danica enter the restaurant. Sue admired Danica's youthful beauty, dressed simply yet elegantly in a white, sleeveless, full-length dress without jewelry. She caught herself staring and returned her gaze to Rob.

"They're here, Rob" Sue took their volume down to a whisper.

"Oh good. This should be fun. Your phone charged for photos?"

"I'm a realtor darling, my phone is always charged for photos."

"A true professional. We're going to have to hope he sits facing us."

"It appears they both will. There's another gentleman with them taking the seat behind you. Your Major Calvert friend."

Rob considered turning around but before he could do so, Calvert placed a hand on Rob's right shoulder.

"Mr. Warner, on holiday I presume?"

Rob recognized Calvert's sardonic voice, always seemingly mocking him. He muttered *shit* under his breath, and half turned his head to look up at Calvert.

"Major. What a surprise." He stood, and noticing Calvert was out of uniform, "Are you on vacation too?"

Instead of answering, Calvert turned his attention to Sue. "Mrs. Warner, I hope you're enjoying your holiday."

"Indeed. We had a lovely train ride through Eastern Europe. Are these your friends?" Sue showed she could lead Calvert in conversation.

"Yes." Calvert turned to introduce Andrei and Danica, who both stood.

"This is Andrei Popov and Danica Ivanova." Andrei walked around the table to shake Sue's hand first, and then Robs'. Danica remained in her spot but smiled warmly.

"Andrei already knows you, Mr. Warner. He purchased your PowerPoint the other day, leading to your attack on the Norfolk Coast Path." Calvert didn't pull his punches.

Rob was never smiling to begin with, but turned his face to a scowl. Calvert had repositioned himself directly in front of Rob and felt him lean forward. He put his hand on Rob's chest and looked him directly in the eyes as he said, "Stand down, Mr. Warner. You need to hear the whole story. Join our table. I'll sit on the end."

***

Sara was seated at dinner with her parents in the pub attached to their hotel. They hadn't stopped apologizing since picking her up from the doughnut at 6 pm, for not arriving sooner. Her mom did all of the talking, although her father could be equally ebullient when discussing his firm's geolocation services tech. He was also a CompSci professor at the University of Texas. Sara sensed he would begin a lecture before the night was over.

Her mom called her Tigger. Sara was grateful the name didn't carry into high school with most of her friends.

"Tigger, I just can't imagine you've been sleeping in that bagel building. How many hours are they making you work?"

"Doughnut mom. They've never given me a work schedule. Just tasks. I don't know when I'm supposed to start each day or when it's okay to go home, but the tasks always seem super urgent, so I work until I finish everything they've given me. And it's just easier to stay there. I have friends there. I drink coffee now."

"That sounds just horrible, Tigger." Her mom flashed an expectant look toward her father as she said this, as if he should do something about it. Her dad remained silent.

"Mom, it's fine, really. I had a motel room, but it's more fun staying in the Doughnut with my new friends. They work so much harder than me, and I'm learning tons. You'd like them, they're so funny. Even when they aren't trying to be, their accents are a hoot. When they hang up a phone call, they say 'cheers, ta-ta for now.' So funny. The last few days have been like being at girl scout camp."

"I assume these ladies are much older?"

"Not by much, mom. They're like college age."

"Well, you'll be staying with us from here on out. This Westin is very nice. Your father will drive you to the Doughnut each morning, and the two of us will pick you up in the evenings. Five o'clock sharp. We'd have been here sooner today, but customs was terribly slow."

"Mom, no way I'll be ready by five. Six would be the earliest. And I like to be there in the morning by 6:30 to join my friends for breakfast. Really, you didn't have to fly out here."

"Yes we did, Tigger. You'll understand why when you're a parent someday. That's nearly a twelve hour day. George, are you going to talk to the major about this?"

"Jenn, please, this is an extraordinary opportunity for Sara. She doesn't appear tired to me."

"Oh, for the love of God in heaven George, listen to yourself. You're a workaholic. Sara is sixteen precious years old. I want you to call that Major Calvert and tell him Sara is coming home."

George and Sara looked at each other. They both knew they intended to ignore Jenn's pleas.

"Listen, the major expects Sara's stay to be a week. Two tops. He'll fly her home, probably before our return trip."

"Why can't she return with us?"

"She doesn't have her passport. She flew here with the military, she needs to return home the same way."

"Is the military paying her for this work?"

George looked to Sara for that answer.

"Major Calvert said I'm still getting paid by Response Software. That I'm on a sort of loan, he uses the term, seconded. And that when I'm done, I'll have a confidential level of security clearance that he says is priceless."

George responded, "For a sixteen-year-old, I'd say it's unheard of. It can easily take a full year just to complete the background checks."

Not trying to joke, Sara said, "Well, maybe sixteen-year-olds have less background to check."

Both parents laughed. Jenn turned her focus to summer vacation conversation, and they enjoyed their family dinner.

***

Back in their hotel room after dinner, while Sara's mom was in the bathroom, her father shared some extra words with her, whispering, which told Sara her mom didn't know what he was about to say.

"Listen, Sara, you should know that I've known Major Calvert for several years. Before we met him at Vegas last year. His team is using my geo-location software."

"So they don't get lost when they're attacking someone?"

George chuckled. "No pumpkin. They generally know where they are. They use my tech to find bad guys. I can't give you any more details than that, but suffice it to say, my firm has more than simply private commercial interests, we work closely with the military. I've known the Major for some time. It's not completely accidental that he responded to your question in Vegas, and eventually found you that summer internship at Response Software. I talk about you every time I meet with him. Point being, Major Calvert is very much aware of you, and he would not expose you to any danger."

"Oh, I know that dad. It is a little weird to be working with all these soldiers, but it's fun at the same time. I have a pool of drivers whenever I need to go anywhere. And I've made some girlfriends here."

"I'm not surprised, pumpkin. Are you aware of the recent NATO exercises in the Baltic States?"

"Yeah, I saw it on my newsfeed, but also, it's been the biggest topic around the Doughnut since it launched."

"Hmm, well, of course, I don't have details on it that I can share, but I will tell you that it's very serious. It's more than a little bit possible that cyberattacks between Russia and the West will escalate as a part of this. So when I said you might be here for two weeks, it could be longer. You shouldn't miss the start of school, I can't see it going that long. You okay with that?"

"Oh dad, absolutely. I wanna stay here as long as they'll have me."

"That's my girl. And careful what you wish for. Night pumpkin." He kissed her on the forehead and sat down in his bed to read his Kindle.

***

Younger people can drink more volume than older people. The five of them quaffed down seven bottles of Vranec wine. Rob felt confident that Calvert and Andrei drank over four of those seven bottles, and Danica out drank Sue. He had twenty years on Calvert and a good thirty over Andrei. He drank half as much, but he'll likely still feel it more than them the next morning.

He only considered the drinking aspect as he thought he might need to split the check after dinner. He liked to use what he termed drinkers' math. He would round the check up to an easy to compute number, divide by the total number of people, then factor by the number of people in each credit card holding party. In this case, round up, divide by five, then factor his portion by two. This math favored drinkers both mentally and financially.

He enjoyed learning about the local wines at dinner. The Lake Ohrid trout was exceptional. And to his surprise, he had one of the most enjoyable evenings in recent memory, sharing cyberwar stores with Andrei. Before dinner, he was prepared to jump across the table and strangle Andrei for being involved in the chain of events that ultimately led to Justin's death.

Sue enjoyed her dinner banter just as much with Danica, gaining insight into the life of an Eastern European fashion model.

Rob and Sue left the three others still sitting at the table to return to their room because fifty-year-olds can't quite hang with drinking twenty-year-olds. Calvert told him not to worry about the dinner bill. They ran into Greg in the lobby as he returned from his dinner.

Sue greeted him. "Greg, you missed quite a dinner here in the hotel."

Greg noticed Sue slurring her words and thought to himself that perhaps he did indeed miss a good time.

"I ran into Private Yankee. We dined down the hill at a place with a deck over the lake. I wouldn't say their trout was better than what I catch fresh in Colorado, but the sauce was unbelievable. A vodka and lemon sauce. I don't think they even tried to cook out the alcohol."

Rob offered his observations on Macedonia. "I suspect this is a drinking country. Doesn't surprise me you ran into Private Yankee."

"Why do you say that?"

"Because Calvert joined us for dinner."

"Ah. Private Yankee wouldn't share any intel. I just assumed he was here following us."

"Sue, Greg and I should probably talk strategy. You can head on up. I'll be up in another thirty minutes."

"You boys talk. I'm done for the night." Sue wobbled toward the elevator.

"Let's sit down over here. Wanna beer?" Greg indicated he was going to order a drink from the lobby bar before they sat down.

"No. Well, sure. A pilsner please."

Rob found them some sofas where they could talk comfortably. He continued where they left off when Greg returned with his draft pilsner.

"So, Triolo wasn't with Yankee?"

"No. That was one of my first questions for Private Yankee. I took the hint from how he avoided an answer and didn't ask any further questions on his operations.

"We talked about my military experience. I shared some stories about Calvert, but he never followed up with anything on the Major. He asked me questions about how I transitioned into the private sector. He's only twenty years old. Barely out of high school. Old enough to drink here but he didn't. Clearly on duty."

"Makes sense. Triolo must still be continuing the ruse of impersonating Calvert so that he could secretly be here."

"He told us that much the other day in Halle, about needing to go dark after purposely maintaining high visibility. He didn't say this is where he was headed. Is he here for Andrei?"

"Exactly. Recruiting him like he did little Sara. He said he's been in contact with Andrei for nearly a year. Sue and I sat at the table with both of them, plus his girlfriend Danica. Calvert's going to transport the two of them into NATO protection."

"Protection from whom?"

"His father for one. His dad is this town's Chief of Police. And his father is essentially on the GRU payroll. So really, he needs protection from the GRU. Andrei says ever since he started his cybercrime operations, he's been the equivalent of an unpaid Russian operative. He was extremely apologetic about our circumstances in the U.K., but he takes his orders from Fancy Bear."

"Interesting. I'm not surprised that's how it works in these countries."

"He's going to request asylum in the U.K. Calvert already has it guaranteed. He's going to work for the Brits at the Doughnut.

And get this. Andrei isn't exactly Guccifer 2.0, but he's close. He said he supplies a good twenty percent of Fancy Bear's botnets."

"No shit?"

"Yeah, of which he figures he loses eighty percent of his potential revenue to the GRU."

"Sounds like he has some financial motivation to leave?"

"He does. He's pretty up-front about that. He's strikingly transparent. But he also insists that if he had legitimate opportunities, he'd like to earn an honest living. He says life in Macedonia is like living as a serf to the Russian nobility. He wants out."

"Interesting. Well, you certainly had the more exciting dinner tonight. And I'm not gonna lie, Sue looked a bit hammered."

"Oh man, so am I. These people can drink."

At this point, Calvert, Andrei, and Danica exited the dining room and greeted Rob and Greg in the lobby.

"Still up, Mr. Warner?"

"I was just bringing Greg up to speed, Major."

"Mr. Foyer, let me introduce you to Mr. Popov and Ms. Ivanova."

Greg was struck by how Andrei Popov looked like a pudgy college frat boy next to the taller and stunningly beautiful Danica Ivanova. He shook hands with the two of them and noticed they both appeared drunk. He wondered if Calvert was too, it didn't show on him.

"I understand you dined with Private Yankee. He pinged me earlier."

"I did. Good kid. He didn't tell me you were here too."

"You didn't have a need to know, Mr. Foyer. I'll be leaving in the morning with Mr. Popov and Ms. Ivanova. I trust you'll be returning by train to Germany for your flights home?"

"That's the plan, Major."

"Try and stick to it. Hope to see you for breakfast. Evening." Calvert said this to the group as he walked toward the elevator. Andrei and Danica stayed behind to talk more with Rob and Greg.

"Would you like a cocktail from the bar, darling?" Andrei asked Danica.

"A brandy would be nice, thank you."

Andrei walked off to get drinks and Danica sat on the couch next to Greg, fanning out her white dress and allowing some of the material to cover Greg's leg. Rob thought about how much this pair could drink while Greg couldn't think of anything to say, like a nerd in high school when the head cheerleader joined him for lunch.

Danica carried the conversation. "The major will be driving us to Kiev tomorrow. We have to leave behind everything. Poor Andrei. He's leaving behind a business that's made him one of the wealthiest men in town. Not to mention a beautiful home overlooking Lake Ohrid."

It occurred to Greg that Calvert would not have shared that intel with them. Rob was able to speak.

"Sounds quite dramatic, Danica. Like a scene out of Casablanca."

She got the reference and smiled, charmed by the thought.

Greg wished he could say something clever like Rob. He remained tongue-tied.

Rob asked, "I imagine you're sacrificing quite a bit yourself?"

"Not really. I do make enough modeling to be independent. Most of my girlfriends, the ones not already married, still live with their parents. But I've made friends with people all over Europe. I believe I have the contacts to get work elsewhere. I hope so."

"I'm sure everything will work out fine. You're both young."

Andrei returned with two brandies, and Rob took the opportunity to excuse himself for the night. *Let these young kids drink. He's done.*

***

Two hours later, 12:03 am as Rob looked at the clock radio LED, he was woken with a start. He was certain he just heard an explosion on the floor beneath him. He could check the hallway but he sensed that might be dangerous. He checked the window instead.

He felt drunk still as he walked over to it. He pulled back the curtain and looked down to the street. He could see the well-lit entrance to the hotel, down to his right. There was no awning and he spotted two men who appeared to be soldiers carrying rifles, or maybe even machine guns. He couldn't make out the weapons precisely, it wasn't his area of expertise, but they were definitely guns.

He then sighted another man walking, more like stumbling, possibly drunk, toward the entrance. Quick as lightning, this third man brandished a handgun and shot the two soldiers with a single round each. They collapsed instantly. The shooter pocketed his gun and picked up one of the soldiers' weapons. Then he entered the hotel. Rob wished he wasn't drunk.

"Sue, wake up!"

***

Greg woke as well to the explosion, and heard the shooting out on the street. Because he stayed up another ninety minutes talking to Andrei and Danica, he'd only been asleep thirty minutes. He immediately dressed and packed. Then he called Rob's mobile.

"Greg, what the fuck?"

"You both ready to go?"

"No. Go where?"

"Dress and pack. Meet me in five minutes downstairs. Take the service elevator down toward your end of the hall, by the ice machine. It lets you out on the first floor in the hallway between the restaurant and the restrooms. There's a back door there. I'll be outside."

Greg hung up and exited into the hallway. He considered taking the stairs rather than the elevator. Then he heard shooting, likely from the lobby. Massive, non-stop shooting, like a pack of a thousand black cat fireworks on the fourth of July. Then it stopped. He felt compelled to investigate, but not via the elevator. He dropped down the stairs and carefully opened the door on the first floor.

First, he smelled the gunpowder. Visibly thick in the air. Nauseating. Then he saw Private Yankee, lying in a pool of red blood on the white tiled floor. He abandoned his caution to rush to his aid.

Greg knelt down over the fallen soldier.

"Private Yankee."

To Greg's relief, the soldier opened his eyes. He began to speak but spit up blood into Greg's face instead.

"Easy son."

"Three of them. Got one of 'em."

Greg looked up to see there was in fact another man lying on the floor of the elevator, his head and arm keeping the door from closing. The stairs were a good call.

"They took the Major. Keys in my pocket to the Major's car. Out back."

Private Yankee spit up more blood, again a direct hit into Greg's face. As Greg wiped the blood from his eyes and looked again at the soldier, Private Yankee was dead. His eyes still open, seemingly looking at Greg to make the next move. He found the keys, then snatched one of the private's dog tags before heading toward the back exit past the restaurant restrooms.

Greg noticed a trail of blood leading to the front door as he walked through the lobby. He was tempted to look out on the front street but stuck to plan and turned down the hallway to the back exit. He used the restroom to wash off the blood and change into a clean t-shirt. The service elevator opened as he exited the restroom. Andrei and Danica emerged carrying backpacks and each with their own cabin-sized suitcase on wheels.

All were equally surprised. Greg spoke first.

"I'm headed out back to meet Rob and Sue. We're taking the Major's car. He's been taken by whomever caused the explosion and shooting."

"I have a car too. Two-seater though."

Danica interjected, "They know your car, darling. It might be better to go with Greg?"

Andrei looked to Greg with a face that suggested he agreed. "Where you going?"

"I don't know. I haven't thought that far ahead yet." The sound of sirens portended the approach of authorities. "Let's walk out back as we talk."

The three saw Rob and Sue already on the sidewalk as they exited the building. No one was sure of what to say. Andrei pointed across the street.

"That's the hotel parking lot. We need to drive to Kiev. What are your plans?"

Greg asked, "What's in Kiev?"

"NATO, and contacts there to get me off the continent."

Rob responded, looking at Greg, "I like the sound of that. How far is Kiev?"

Andrei replied, "We could probably drive straight through, but I've always stopped for the night in Satu Mar when I've driven it previously. It's a two-day drive. Let's drive that far at least. It's in Romania, very near the Ukraine border. We can stop there and reassess if we want to continue into Ukraine."

Greg pushed the electronic button on the Major's keys and saw the lights flash on a Volvo SUV. "The Major's car looks like it could hold all of us. We all in agreement? Kiev by way of Satu Mar?"

The group nodded in affirmation and quickly boarded the car in silence, well aware that they needed to exit the scene before the police arrived to discover them fleeing from the back of the hotel. Greg took the wheel. Rob suggested Andrei ride shotgun to navigate as he was the local. Rob, Sue, and Danica sat in the rear bench seat. Andrei typed Satu Mar into the nav screen and Greg led them out of town, away from the bloody hotel scene. He began the conversation after the sirens had muted.

"I'm glad none of you had to see the scene in the hotel lobby. It was a pool of blood. Private Yankee died just as I reached him. He gave me these keys. He told me the Major had been captured. He killed one of them. Some guy wearing fatigues."

Andrei offered his insight. "If he was actually in uniform, he was probably the Macedonian Army. We're not part of NATO, not yet. But fatigues alone don't mean a uniform. Just as likely he was Russian GRU. Or Macedonian Army acting on their behalf. Trust me, this town is as good as Russian territory. We need to get out of here before roadblocks are erected."

Rob joined in. "What about the Major?" No one responded, but Greg sighed audibly. "Greg, I saw a man shoot two soldiers, at least they looked like soldiers, and enter the hotel. Now that I think about it, that was probably Private Yankee. He was trying to protect the Major."

Sue overcame her shock enough to speak. "Rob, what are you saying? These are soldiers. We have to leave."

Greg responded, "I don't know how we'd track them Rob. I mean, I'm with you. I'd go after them if I knew where to look."

Andrei knew where to look.

"Greg, turn left here. Drive slow and park on the right, just at the corner two blocks down."

Danica knew where Andrei was headed. "Andrei no. We can't go there."

Sue trusted talking to Danica more than the men. "Where?"

"The city police station."

Andrei responded to calm the women down. "We won't go near it. I'll get out and look around the corner. Just to see if there's anything going on."

Before anyone could contest this plan, Greg reached the corner and stopped. Andrei got out walked far enough to peer past the corner of the building down the side street. After ten seconds, he returned to the car.

"Turn back around and get back on course out of town."

Rob responded while Greg focused on driving. "What'd you see?"

"A couple of SUVs parked out front and a half dozen men in fatigues. Didn't look like they were displaying military insignias. They were Russian. They own my dad's station. He basically works for them. Probably more by choice than I do. I can guarantee you, the Major is in that jail."

Sue asked, "But we're leaving, right?"

"Yes baby, don't worry. I'm not crazy, we're not breaking Calvert of out of some jail."

Greg added, "But if we know where he is, we can probably do something. Communicate to someone."

Rob responded, "I'm calling little Sara. She's practically living with NATO. She can notify someone."

Rob noticed that he'd picked up the Major's habit of applying the term little to Sara's name. That made him feel better somehow, like he was on Calvert's side.

***

"Sara. Answer your phone."

Sara's dad was the only one woken by the ringing of Sara's phone on the nightstand. The three of them shared a room with two double beds at the Westin.

Sara had unique ringtones for everyone important at work, so she knew it was Rob as she answered on speakerphone.

"Sir?" Less than a week working at the Doughnut and she even called her dad sir now.

"Sara, listen."

"I am."

"Can you let me speak to a military officer?"

Sara looked at the time on her phone. "Sir, I don't know where you are, but it's 11:30 at night here."

"Oh. Yeah. I'm an hour ahead of you Sara. Listen, this is very important. How quickly could you contact your NATO officers?"

"I have some of them in my contacts. I could text you their information if you want to call them yourself?"

"Perfect. Who's the highest ranking officer you know?"

"Major Calvert. You know him right?"

"I do Sara, but I need someone else. Who else do you know that's pretty high up?"

"I have a guy he works closely with. Major Fitzmaurice. He's British, is that okay?"

"Perfect, can you ping me that right now?"

"I just did."

"Got it. Thanks Sara. Sorry for waking you. Goodnight."

"Cheers. Ta-ta for now."

Rob hung up, too focused to notice the British accent Sara affected as she said goodbye. He dialed Major Fitzmaurice who answered on the second ring.

"Major Fitzmaurice."

"Sir, this is Rob Warner. Sorry if I've woken you. I'm a friend of Major Calvert."

"I know who you are, Mr. Warner. Proceed."

Rob wasn't surprised the Major knew him and filed that thought away to consider the significance for later. He quickly and correctly assumed though that he could take some shortcuts in his explanation of events.

"Sir, Major Calvert was captured in a shootout at the Hotel Belvedere in Lake Ohrid, Macedonia. Private Yankee was killed trying to save him. It appears the abduction of Major Calvert was the objective, and we strongly believe he is being held in the Lake Ohrid City Police Station."

"How strongly?"

"Ninety-nine percent, sir. We didn't see him but we did confirm a large group of men in fatigues, whom Andrei believes to be Russian, posted in front of the police station after the attack."

"What time was the attack, Mr. Warner?"

"Roughly thirty minutes ago. Just after midnight, CET."

"Thank you for the readout, Mr. Warner. Can you describe for me your position? Where are you and who are you with?"

"I'm driving north out of town, on our way to Satu Mar, Romania. Our ultimate destination is Kiev. I'm with my wife, Sue, my business partner Greg Foyer, and Andrei Popov and his girlfriend Danica Ivanova."

"I see." The Major paused momentarily. "Proceed to Satu Mar. If you're not comfortable with that, I can suggest a couple of places in Macedonia."

"I'm fine. I don't think any of us trust stopping in Macedonia."

"Exactly my thoughts too, Mr. Warner. The original plan was for Calvert and Andrei to rendezvous at another site in Romania and to helicopter into Kiev. You won't be able to cross the Ukrainian border. It will be totally shut down by the time you reach it. I'll redirect the transport to the city airport in Satu Mar and meet you there personally. I'll text you more detailed instructions in the next hour. Can you do that?"

"Yes, sir. We should be in Satu Mar by noon."

Andrei interjected. "More likely before 10 am. Maybe 8:00."

"Make that between 8 and 10 am, Major."

"Very good, Mr. Warner. Understand it's very important we have Andrei in Kiev within the next twenty-four hours. He knows why. Please ping me hourly of your progress at this number."

"Will do, Major. Thank you."

"Thank you, sir. Good luck."

***

They crossed into Romania after less than four hours of driving. They had to show their passports at a border checkpoint, but there were no questions and it took less than two minutes. They took the opportunity to refuel at a nearby gas station, and to stretch their legs. While Greg stood at the pump, the rest of them entered the convenience style store.

Rob bought the coffee, more for the game he liked to play transacting in foreign currencies than generosity. It was his tourist exercise. He bought one each for all five passengers, and carried them over to Andrei who was watching a news channel while the women used the restroom. Rob recognized the scene but couldn't read the text scrolling across the screen.

"That looks like the Belvedere Hotel?"

"It is. They were just showing the police station. Oh, there it is again. I wish they'd turn on the volume."

Rob didn't need the volume. And he didn't need to interpret the language. The police station was in flames, and numerous dead bodies were visible in the street. He could guess what happened.

"They say who attacked the police station?"

"NATO. They're saying it's unconfirmed still by our own army, so there's still quite a bit of confusion. It's just all unanswered questions. Why would the military attack the police? Why would it be NATO instead of our own army? Was our army operating as part of NATO?   Who attacked the hotel and is there a connection?"

"Hmm. Glad they aren't asking us."

Andrei took Rob's comment as American humor and they shared a nervous laugh.

"Yeah, glad we crossed that border."

The news scene switched to a map of Europe, including Russia.

"What are they saying now?"

"Hard to really know without the volume on but based on the text, I'd guess they're making references to World War I. They always do.   It could just be farmers going on strike and they reference World War I. It's like they want it to happen again, and for it to start here. I don't understand why but the media always plays that up."

"Hmm. It's not an unusual reference back home, depending on the events. I wouldn't think the NATO war games in the Baltics would be that big a deal."

"It is. They're showing that now. I'll bet you a Euro they'll show Ukraine next?"

Rob was tempted to take the bet to continue his game of currency transactions, but the scene switched to Ukraine before he could reply. The women exited the restroom, and Rob handed Sue the coffee tray so he could take his turn. Rob noted that Andrei never took a turn, even after Greg did. *Young people.* He asked Andrei about it once they started driving again.

"You get a chance to use the restroom, Andrei?"

"Oh, I went before we left the hotel. I can hold it all day. I know, it's not so easy as you age is it?"

"Oh man, now that we're drinking coffee, it's more like managing a slow leak."

The car erupted in laughter and the traveling group shared stories, developing a cross-generational bond over the remaining drive to Satu Mar. Rob avoided sharing the news he and Andrei watched in the store to keep from worrying the women. He suspected lowering the intensity level was equally good for himself.

***

They arrived at Satu Mar shortly after 9 am and followed the detailed instructions Major Fitzmaurice texted to Rob's phone. Their route had them go through an entrance guarded by the Romanian military, who directed them to a small jet on the tarmac.

The soldiers on the ground guided them to board the craft. Greg handed them the rental car keys.

Inside was Major Fitzmaurice, who greeted them with the warmest smile he could muster for civilians, but he hadn't slept in the last thirty hours.

"Ladies, I'm Major Fitzmaurice. You must be Sue."

"Yes, pleased to meet you, Major."

"Likewise, and you must be Danica." He shook their hands and directed them to take their seats.

"Gentlemen, Major Fitzmaurice." He shook each man's hands.

"Rob Warner, Major."

"Greg Foyer, sir."

"Andrei Popov."

"Andrei, please take a seat in the back. I'll join you momentarily so we can discuss our next steps during the flight."

Rob tried to steal the Major's attention, before what would obviously be an immediate takeoff.

"Major, can you give us a readout on Major Calvert?"

"We have him back Mr. Warner, thanks to your quick and accurate intel. I understand he's been wounded, and that's all the details I have. I expect we'll see him in Kiev."

"Were his attackers Russian?"

"Sorry, Mr. Warner. That's operational intelligence. Buckle up."

Chapter Ten

"SASHA, give me a readout on Andrei."

"Special Ops failed to capture him, Mr. President. Their operations in the hotel were interrupted by a gunfight. When they returned for him, he was already gone. We assume he left with the other Americans. He left his pricey Italian sports car behind."

"Will he return for it?"

"No, sir. He's too young and rich to understand the value of money."

"Can Andrei hurt us?"

"Besides the wind farm operation, he controls most of Ukraine's critical infrastructure."

"Anything in the Baltics?"

"No, sir, that's primarily run out of Kaliningrad and Minsk."

"Good. Our focus needs to be the Baltics. Ukraine can wait for after the Baltic war games. Instruct our friends to close out their energy positions. I consider the wind farm operation a success, based on advanced orders for Nord Stream II."

"Thank you, Sir. I'll wind it down. Of course, with Andrei gone, the malware campaign is essentially dead in the water already."

"You think that's why Calvert was after Andrei?"

"No, sir. He just learned of the wind farm attack six days ago. This is either a longer-term plan to steal our hybrid war assets, or his objective is Ukraine. Or both."

"When Andrei surfaces, extract his access credentials to all

Ukrainian assets and kill him."

"Yes, sir."

"The gunships that rescued Major Calvert, Macedonia military?"

"NATO, launched from Kiev, sir."

"That's unacceptable, Sasha."

"That NATO is involved, sir?   Or operating from these countries?"

"That NATO even exists. NATO doesn't matter in the course of history, Sasha. But yes, these are not NATO member countries. This is unparalleled aggression."

"Agreed, sir. I'll prepare plans for you to take action in Ukraine as soon as the Baltic exercises complete, sir."

"Does it make sense to return some of our forces back to the Donetsk and Luhansk borders now?"

"Yes. It will take several days. We could reinforce the region quicker with fresh troops rather than return them from the Baltics."

"No, too expensive. If something happens, we have our forces in Crimea. I'll send the order later this morning."

Putin hung up.

***

"Good morning, Miss Thomas."

"Captain Jefferies, morning sir."

"The wind farm operation is complete, Miss Thomas. Major Calvert is extremely pleased with your contribution."

"Thank you, sir. Are you sending me home?"

"Do you want to go home?"

"School doesn't start for another two weeks, sir. I'd like to stay. Can you send my parents home?"

Jefferies laughed. "I'll look into it, Miss Thomas. I want you to move your gear into Captain Burke's area. I understand you've been bunking with some of her troops here in the Doughnut."

"I was sir, until my parents showed up."

"Well, now you're on their team. Private James here will help you move. Your clearance has been increased to grant you access. Captain Burke will explain your new assignment to you. The assignment's expected to last forty-eight hours. Call your parents now, before you learn the assignment details. Tell them you won't be leaving here tonight, but you can expect to return to the States, Saturday morning. I'll be on that flight to escort you home."

"Thank you, sir."

"Thank you, Miss Thomas."

***

The NATO jet ferrying Rob and his holiday tourists slash business team slash group of exiles toward Kiev could fit two adjacent seats per side. Instead, it was configured with single, plush leather seats, facing each other in sets with small tables in between. The downside of this configuration was there were no leg rests. Rob and Greg sat facing each other, with the two ladies across the aisle. They leaned toward each other with elbows on the table, speaking low so that the women couldn't hear them.

"So the man I saw shoot two soldiers outside at the entrance, pick up one of their guns and enter the hotel. That was Private Yankee?"

"Right. I found him with an AK-12, a very modern Russian assault rifle. He took out one of the men half inside the elevator. I suspect at least one other was shot based on the trail of blood leading to the front door."

"Could have been Calvert," Rob said.

"Yeah. Sounds like he's okay though."

"Well, he's alive. That Major Fitzmaurice doesn't expound much on a story."

"Yeah. I get that, I mean, sensitive intel and we're on the outside."

"Sure." Rob asked, "What do you think he's doing in the back with Andrei?"

"Well, clearly Andrei knew the plan before he arrived. He didn't speak to any of that on our drive. He's key to whatever comes next."

"I've heard you talk Greg, about him being Guccifer 2.0. You still think that?"

"It makes sense that he could be involved. He's close to Fancy Bear. But the prevailing thought is Guccifer 2.0 is one, a digital persona and not a single, real person. And two, that the persona is comprised of GRU officers. What Andrei is, what we know, is that he runs a very successful dark net marketplace, and he's leveraged by the GRU."

"Hey, you never told me. Were you able to breach any of Andrei's systems in his room?"

"Oh, man. Everything's been happening so fast. The rooms were too big for me to even see a Bluetooth signal, well accept for

Danica's mobile but that wasn't useful. I did hack into the hotel's wifi though."

"How'd you do that?"

"Standard stuff really. Off-the-shelf tools. Very involved though, lots of steps. I didn't have time to look for vulnerabilities on his systems before the shooting started.

"I used the Jens Steube WPA2 attack. I was able to get the EAPOL frame from the wifi server. I got that using the hcxdumptool. I outputted that to a hash, then obtained the pre-shared key via Hashcat. So I owned the network with all off-the-shelf stuff. If they'd have logged into anything unencrypted, I could have sniffed their traffic, but I didn't have time for that. No doubt Andrei always hits a VPN proxy first, but sometimes even the most security-conscious find themselves in a hurry. I needed another day."

"What's our plan, Rob? I would think, now that you and Andrei are drinking buddies, our work here is done. Time to go home."

"We're not drinking buddies. Don't start with that. But sure, I agree. Probably time to go home. I'd like to enjoy a few more days here, but we have to be home by Monday so Sue can be with Ella for an OBGYN visit."

"She pregnant?"

"No, not anymore. Long story."

"Oh, sorry Rob. We don't have to discuss it."

"No, it's fine. I'll tell you in the right setting."

"So, we land in Kiev and rebook our flights?"

"I might look into a train back to Germany. Sue likes trains."

***

Early afternoon CET, the jet landed in Kiev. Andrei was still absorbed in whatever activity he'd been performing the entire flight on his laptop. Rob and Greg also processed some work email, after discovering the jet had wifi. Major Fitzmaurice escorted them off the jet with instructions for what he expressed as their options.

"Andrei needs to spend a few hours here on the base finishing up his activities with my team. I don't have an exact ETA, but we'll be taking the jet to Cheltenham this evening. Danica, you'll be traveling with us. Mr. and Mrs. Warner, and Mr. Foyer, you're welcome to ride along. If not, the private here will transport you to the commercial entry of this airfield. You can also catch a train there."

Rob looked over to Sue.

"Sue, I thought we could maybe take a train back to Germany?"

"That's sweet of you darling, but I'd like to get back home to Ella as soon as possible."

Major Fitzmaurice said, "I highly suggest you all take the flight I'm offering. I can't go into details, but border security will be tight. You might run into troubles exiting the country by train."

Greg responded. "Will you be serving peanuts, Major? I don't recall having either breakfast or lunch yet."

The group laughed, and Rob seconded Greg's thoughts. "We'll take you up on your offer, Major. Can you suggest a place for us to grab a late lunch while we wait? And can we just leave our bags here then?"

"You might want to carry them with you, Mr. Warner. You'll have a chance to shower and change on the base. Major Calvert is waiting for you to join him in the mess hall. I'll escort you. You'll find the food surprisingly good. And they serve a local craft pilsner. I understand you're somewhat of a beer aficionado."

"I am indeed, Major. Greg, remind me to delete my Facebook account." Rob was only half-joking.

All Greg heard was the part about Major Calvert as they were close friends. "Did you say Major Calvert is here?"

"Yes, he'd like to debrief you on last night's events in Lake Ohrid. Follow me."

The mess hall became obvious as they walked toward the main building. There was an outdoor seating area, not unlike a beer garden, offering views of the massive concrete tarmac, replete with hanging flower baskets. Rob couldn't fault them for trying to add the comfort touches. They entered the mess hall to discover a beer hall atmosphere with picnic tables, easily a hundred soldiers, and a quick-serve concept buffet line.

Major Fitzmaurice placed a call on his mobile. "Major Calvert. Where are you seated? Oh yes, yes, I see you. We'll join you after getting our food. Cheers."

No one else saw Calvert, but they followed the Major through the food line and ultimately to a picnic table where Major Calvert was the only patron, notable considering how full the mess hall was.

Greg considered giving the Major a hug but held off after seeing his right arm in a sling.

"Major Calvert, I can't tell you how relieved I am to see you in one piece." Greg was surprised with himself at how emotional he felt.

"I feel the same way, Greg. About all of you. Please, sit down, and I'll give you a readout on what happened, to the extent I can based on your need to know."

The group sat down together for their first meal in nearly twenty hours. Rob shook Calvert's hand before sitting down across from him. He was sensitive to how Sue might be feeling, seeing Calvert was injured after just eating dinner with him the previous night. He started the conversation lightly.

"No beer, Major? This pilsner is excellent. Quite fresh. Strong hops for a pils."

"Muscle relaxers. Mixing with alcohol is not recommended."

"Ah. You get shot in the arm during the attack?"

"No, the ceiling caved in on me during my rescue. I did get shot twice though by Private Yankee in my right side. Just flesh wounds. If I were drinking, I'd offer a toast to that brave soldier."

Rob and Greg both nodded toward Major Fitzmaurice to affirm they shared Calvert's sentiment. The mood was now full-on serious.

Sue addressed her concerns. "Major, please don't take this the wrong way. I'm very relieved to see you're relatively okay, but I have to say, in the last twenty-four hours, I feel as if I've gone from a romantic European vacation to a war zone."

"That's fair, and not totally inaccurate, Mrs. Warner. I'll share what I can." Calvert wished he had a beer. He noticed Rob take a large swig after his wife spoke to the elephant in the room.

"You met Private Triolo in Germany and spent some time with him as part of my operation doppelgänger. The purpose of that mission was for me to stealth travel to Lake Ohrid to offer Andrei immunity in the U.K.

"Turns out, Andrei is a closely monitored Russian asset. I wasn't there twenty-four hours. That the Russians abducted me is arguably an act of war." Calvert looked at Fitzmaurice as he said this. "Maybe this is a casus belli, but could be useful in the days ahead."

Fitzmaurice grunted a thoughtful concurrence.

Rob asked it before Sue could respond. "Major, are you suggesting we *are* in a war zone now?"

"You'll be flying out with me tonight to the U.K. before

hostilities break out. That's as much as I can speak on the topic. And you're not to speak to anyone on this topic before tomorrow. No emails. No phone calls."

"Understood."

Sue was not so sure she understood but decided she should follow Rob's lead and defer to Calvert's authority. Danica was much more submissive, afraid to say anything that might jeopardize either Andrei's plans for their asylum, or whatever else plans he might have made with this Major Calvert. Greg was still curious.

"How'd you confirm they were Russian, Major? If you can say."

"They were speaking German after they flash-bombed my door and attacked me in my room. Once Private Yankee started shooting at them in the elevator, they quickly switched to Russian."

"I saw the guy he killed in the elevator. Private Yankee thought he might have injured another one of them?"

"He shot all three. And me. We heard his two shots when he took out the guards. They were ready for him, but he really had us at a disadvantage in that elevator. My two surviving abductors nearly bled out before we made it to the police station a few blocks away. I doubt they lived."

"Andrei's father make himself visible?"

"He introduced himself to me with a punch to my gut." Calvert wanted to follow this up by looking at Andrei and saying 'class move,' but held back because he later saw Andrei's dad dead on the floor as he exited the building. He'd share that with him later.

Rob rejoined the conversation. "Major, I'm having trouble connecting any of this to the NATO war games in the Baltics, let alone as a counterattack for the wind farm cyber breaches?"

"Those connections exceed your need to know, Mr. Warner. I will tell you though the wind farm attacks have been effectively countered, much to little Sara's credit, mind you. Not sure how that positions you for further consulting work." Calvert was back to form with responses that Rob found more confrontational than informative.

"Good to know, Major."

***

The Americans were able to shower and change after lunch. Calvert left with Fitzmaurice and Andrei to complete whatever activities Andrei was committed to perform. Before dark, the original crew plus Calvert were back on board the jet and headed for the U.K. The seating arrangements were different on this leg with Rob sitting with Sue, Andrei with Danica, and Greg with Calvert. Major Fitzmaurice was paired with the private.

It's not often, but also not unusual for Sue to tag along with Rob on business trips this last year since he'd become a partner in Response Software. This was Sue's first international travel with Rob on business though. It didn't turn out as she'd imagined. She talked soft enough to where she believed the sound of the jet's engines would keep others from hearing their conversation.

She asked, "Do you think the Major slipped when he told us we'd be out before the hostilities started?"

"That's exactly what I thought. He didn't mean to tell us that. Muscle relaxers."

"So, what hostilities, Rob? Is America going to attack Russia?"

"No, no, nothing quite that dramatic. I think worse case, NATO could be involved. Well actually, considering what we know, clearly NATO is involved. But he was referencing Ukraine. Even Fitzmaurice said earlier that the Ukrainian border security would be tight. And it's fair to say Ukraine is already at war with the Separatists. A civil war of sorts. I suspect the government might be launching an offensive against the Separatists."

"I didn't know Ukraine was a member of NATO?"

"I don't know if they are or not. I don't follow the news as much as you, Sue. If you think about it, they can't be. Otherwise, the Russian attack on Crimea would have triggered Article 5 and we'd have all been at war."

"Good point," Sue said. "That airbase though had an awful lot of NATO uniforms. Something's up."

"I noticed that too. I was talking to a NATO officer in the shower. We had a TV monitor playing CNN. Not sure about your locker room but the men's was fairly upscale, like at a nice golf club or spa."

"Yes, mine was very nice. And it almost was a spa. It was next to a hair salon. I'm beginning to think the military lifestyle isn't so bad."

"Calvert seems to like it. Anyway. This NATO officer was British, so he spoke English. The volume was turned off on the TV, but he told me the story was on the NATO helicopter attack on the police station in Lake Ohrid. And that combined with our war games in the Baltics, Russia was ratcheting up the rhetoric. He said we could expect the fallout would likely be in Ukraine."

"Why does Russia care? I would think it should be Macedonia that would be upset."

"That's exactly what I said. He told me that, with the exception of Ukraine, I should consider any non-NATO country to be the same as Russia. I guess that statement confirms Ukraine is not a NATO member too. He said the government of Macedonia leans toward NATO, but their culture is Slavic and Russia maintains a strong presence. He might have been exaggerating, but believe me Sue, had I known that, I wouldn't have taken you to Macedonia. I'm very sorry about that."

"Oh Rob, I'm fine. I'm not upset over that. I mean, I got a little spooked when Major Calvert suggested hostilities would be starting, but I truly enjoyed our Eastern European train ride adventure. Now that we're safe, our exit from the hotel, and drive into Romania was quite thrilling. I'll travel anywhere with you dear."

"Hmm. Well thanks. That was a nice train ride."

"I've been meaning to ask. How's your little tummy injury?"

"Fine. It didn't get in the way of my performance the other night on the train."

"Rob. Keep your voice down." Sue looked around at the other passengers.

***

Greg and Calvert were seated across the aisle from Rob and Sue and too involved in their own conversation to overhear anyone else.

"Listen Greg, I sort of expect Andrei to tell you everything he's been doing. He's not military, so my plan with him is to keep him as isolated from the general population as possible. I'll share with you what I suspect you've already inferred based on what you've seen.

"Andrei is helping us to one, close the breaches in Ukraine's critical infrastructure so they aren't exposed to a counterattack by Russia as part of a hybrid war campaign. He's essentially completed those actions.

"Two, he's currently weaponizing breaches to the eastern regions of Ukraine, Donetsk and Luhansk, which are largely controlled by the Separatists. Ukraine will copy a page from General Gerasimov's handbook on hybrid warfare and cripple their critical infrastructure before launching a full-on military counteroffensive to retake their country. Cyber operations will begin tonight after midnight."

"Jesus. And NATO is involved?"

"You'd be surprised to learn just how involved, but I can't talk about that. I will say, we won't be directly part of offensive operations, because that would be like directly attacking Russia. The separatist's ranks are bolstered by Russian troops."

"The attack in Lake Ohrid wasn't directly against Russia?"

"Well, we can, and in fact are saying that they attacked us first when they abducted me. Any other time that might be a big issue, but by this time tomorrow, no one will remember that Charlie Foxtrot."

"This feels dangerous. Almost reckless for NATO."

"It is dangerous. NATO is taking an aggressive stance to send a signal to Russia to back off on their election meddling and all their other geopolitical shit. We're going to show them that there are consequences to their actions, by retaking Eastern Ukraine. Anything less from us is just toothless rhetoric.

"I'm sharing this with you to enlist your help in ensuring Mr. Warner goes home with his wife. That boy has a history of getting himself in over his head. This is cyberwar Greg, not cybercrime. There's a real difference. Cyberwar will get you killed."

"I'll get Rob and Sue home."

***

Andrei and Danica caught up on the last twenty-four hours in their conversation.

"Will we ever be able to return home, Andrei?"

"Not for some time darling. If ever. I never knew how closely the Russians were keeping tabs on me. The Major told me my father died in the rescue attack on his police station. I won't be able to attend his funeral."

"Oh baby. I didn't know that. Are you okay?"

"It's a lot to take in. I'm not sure how I feel. I've been thinking of my mother and little brother."

"You think they're in danger?"

"I don't have any reason to think that, but then I had no idea I was under constant surveillance. I need to get money to them. If possible, I'd like them to join us. You never know."

"I'll work on that as soon as we land, darling. They can live with us."

"Thanks baby."

"I don't want you worrying. You keep focused on what you have to do." Danica paused. "Andrei, can you tell me what it is you're doing? For Major Calvert?"

"Well." Andrei raised his head and stared at the ceiling of the plane for a moment, determining how to best share his story with Danica. She was a fashion model, but was also an advanced math student in high school and knew a thing or two about computers.

"I think sharing this with you is okay, darling. Let me start with some context. You remember last month's NotPetya cyberattack? On Constitution Day."

"How could I forget? It was a massive ransomware attack that shut down the entire country. I was in Italy and couldn't get home for nearly a week."

"Right. It was massive. But it wasn't a ransomware attack. Petya was a ransomware attack, from a year or so ago. NotPetya was like a ransomware attack, but it didn't ask for a ransom. Its damage was irreversible. It was otherwise the same codebase. That's why it was called *Not*Petya. It was essentially the Petya malware, but it wasn't used as ransomware."

"I'm following."

"Well, I'm the guy who was responsible for the original Petya."

"You wrote Petya? Darling, I'm impressed."

"Thanks baby. To be honest, I bought it, but I improved it dramatically before launching it. That malware campaign is where I made most of my money."

"About the time you started wining and dining me."

"Yes, well, pretty much. Anyway, it was also when Fancy Bear got his hooks into me. The General recruited me," Andrei used air quotes, "to modify Petya for what became NotPetya."

"You did that? Andrei." Danica gave Andrei a disapproving look, that on her face was such a sexy pout that Andrei would consider telling her more bad news just to watch. "That was so bad."

"I know, but first, I had no choice. And second, I didn't really do much. I provided the malware and trained this Sandworm team to use it. A bunch of Russian military types. Sandworm modified it and launched it. So it wasn't really me."

"OK, I understand. I know how they've been using you through your father. I'm still so sorry, darling."

"Thanks, baby. So, with that as context, this Major Calvert, who has contacted me several times over the last year, shows up at my office two days ago, my home, and tells me how he knows everything about me, and asks me if I'd like to work for the good guys. I figured you'd be much happier if I wasn't an international criminal and I agreed to his plan."

"Living in the U.S. rather than Russia, yes, but his plan being?"

"Launch a much-improved derivative of NotPetya against the Separatists. Tonight. As soon as we land actually. He has this woman, he calls her little Sara, who's been coding a library of IP addresses that will contain the blast radius of this attack to the Donetsk and Luhansk regions."

"Blast radius?"

"Yeah, that's how the Major talks. The problem with NotPetya was that, although it was targeted at Ukraine, it quickly spread around the globe. The General made me the fall guy in the Kremlin when it took down Rosneft. That was totally those Sandworm fuckups."

"No doubt, baby. Is that why you agreed so quickly to work for Major Calvert?"

"No, I wasn't really in trouble with the Kremlin. That was just another way of the General getting his hooks into me deeper. I had different reasons. One is that I really would like to be legit. The other is how bad I felt about Rob Warner and his partner who got killed."

"What happened?"

"I set up Warner's team to be attacked by the GRU. I didn't know the General would try to kill them. I expected them to steal their laptops. Rob doesn't understand how well-known he is in my circles. He might seem to you as such an average guy, but to people like me, he's a hero. You couldn't even get close to him last year at DEF CON with everyone buying him drinks at the bar. The guy's a rockstar in cybersecurity."

"What does he do?"

"Nothing normally. He's just your typical corporate knucklehead managing a team of forensic analysts to research cyberattacks. But when he was confronted with a cyberattack last year with the potential to set the world back into the digital dark ages, he stepped up. I mean, depending on who you talk to, he either broke a bunch of laws that should have landed him in prison. He did lose his job.

Or you could say he put his life on the line and stopped a nuclear war.

"There's more than a few conspiracy theories floating around, but he's basically a hero in my industry and I contributed to almost killing him. I feel obligated to make it up to him."

"That's why I love you, baby. So, Ukraine is launching a cyberattack against the Separatists tonight?"

"Well, actually, I am. I own the attack vector. A software company that makes the tax software called M.E.Doc that everyone in Ukraine uses. I used them for NotPetya, by infecting their software update servers. They think they cleaned up my backdoor by rebuilding all their systems. What they don't know is my backdoor was actually a person, a key firewall admin on their staff. Instead of blaming their systems, they should have fired everyone. He built me another backdoor as soon as they reinstalled their network.

"After I get little Sara's code, I'll update NotPetya 2 and weaponize the same software update servers I used before. I just need a single vulnerable PC to be online and this thing will spread like wildfire in a matter of minutes."

Chapter Eleven

THE clouds at ten thousand feet unveiled a gorgeous sunset during the crew's descent over England, making darkness rather sudden as they deplaned at 10 pm. A short drive later to Cheltenham deposited the women at the Westin Hotel, with the men ending their journey at the Government Communications Headquarters - GCHQ - also known as the Doughnut.

"Mr. Warner, I'll give you exactly ten minutes to communicate with Little Sara, then the private here will return you to your wife for a late dinner at the Westin. Sara has a full night of work ahead of her." Calvert wasn't happy with Rob's insistence at checking in on Sara's welfare. He suspected Rob had a hidden agenda.

"I'm pretty sure making her work through the night violates Texas State children work laws."

"Oh, you're suddenly an expert on employment law?"

"I assume I'm paying her wages here. Seriously Major, why are you making her work so hard?" Rob was sincerely interested in how Sara was doing. He wanted to express this to her, something bred into him from his years as a manager of young employees.

"I'll be honest with you, Mr. Warner, that girl is a prodigy. Her skills querying big data for intelligence are nothing short of magic. She learns new systems that would take months for an average person, quite literally in minutes. She works twelve hour days and finds time to finish reading a new paperback, almost daily. I would peg Little Sara's IQ at maybe 180. And she's loving this work."

"Hmm. Why do you always call her little?"

"Have you ever seen her eat? She must weigh only ninety pounds and I swear I've watched her eat twenty pounds for breakfast. The girl is a miracle in human biology."

Rob chuckled. "Yeah, now that you mention it, I took her to lunch once when she first hired on. She asked me if we could order a second appetizer."

Rob and Calvert shared a laugh as they entered the building and passed Security.

***

Rob and Sara talked only briefly. Rob hoped Sara would join him and Sue on their return flight but learned she would instead be traveling home on a military transport. Something about arriving without a passport. Sara told Rob that, based on a text she just received from her mom, Sue was currently having a late dinner with Sara's parents and that Rob was invited to join them. Rob took the hint and let her return to her work.

This left Sara with Andrei. At the same time, a private arrived and provided Andrei access credentials to join the wifi. Andrei handed Sara a USB drive.

"Can you copy your code to that?"

"Sure." Sara attached the drive to her workstation. "Are you going to add it to your Notpetya code?"

"Not exactly. Notpetya is the encryption software. It's the package that will be delivered by another piece of code which is a variant of EternalBlue."

"The NSA malware?"

"Exactly. Thank you team U.S.A."

"My dad told me that's the problem with government involvement in cyberwar. Once they've released an attack into the wild, it becomes available for the bad guys to use."

"Exactly. Not that I'm not grateful, but they should really put some more thought into their actions." Andrei typed on his keyboard while chatting with Sara, logging into his VPN and launching multiple programs. "How'd you code your library of IP addresses?"

"It's just a text file, in a little Ruby-on-Rails wrapper." Sara handed the USB drive back to Andrei.

"Perfect." Andrei attached the drive to his laptop. "Thank you. How'd you get this list?"

"The military has access to everything. Different databases but I

116

got access to domain name registrars for Eastern European critical infrastructure, ISPs, telcos, you name it, plus a private IP profile database they maintain here. I cross-referenced everything with the most powerful geo-IP location-based services I've ever seen. CyberCom has it all."

"Hmm."

"How are you going to keep it from spreading all over the world?"

"I'm not. I'm still going to allow it to spread, but I'll only activate it against the IP address ranges in your text file. It's a more efficient approach."

Andrei had less than two hours to prepare for his attack, so he took shortcuts. He found he was able to effectively task Sara to perform some of the work. He'd be ready to meet the Major's timeline.

***

There was no rational reason for the mood to be celebratory, but several attendees gathered in the morning in the Westin lobby to see Sara off for her flight home felt a sense of accomplishment. Rob had been up since 4 am in the lounge with Sara's parents watching CNN coverage of fighting in Ukraine.

Government forces began an intense ground and air counteroffensive against the Separatists at 2 am CET. Reporting suggested defensive measures were severely hampered by a tactic termed hybrid warfare. Surprisingly, NATO was quick to go on record with their involvement to state they were leading cyber offensive operations from Cheltenham, effectively disabling all power and communications in the Donetsk and Luhansk regions.

NATO further announced troop deployments along the Ukrainian border with Crimea, to fence off Russian troops stationed there, allowing offensive Ukraine operations to focus on the Separatists. Apparently other Russian troops in the area had redeployed to their borders with the Baltics, lured there by Operation Nerf Ball. The Ukraine counteroffensive was expected to be over in hours, days before Russia could effectively respond. NATO might have some explaining to do at the U.N., but there was little Russia could do now to turn back the tide.

Sara's parents were proud of her involvement, as was Rob. Nothing would bring back Justin, but his team played a part in the response, even if unrelated to the wind farm breach, against the bad actors behind Justin's murder. He was glad he stayed in Europe to see this thing through.

He was giving Sara a bear hug, looking out through the glass turnstile, when he saw the two soldiers sitting in the jeep intended to drive Sara to the airbase, virtually explode in a bloody barrage of automatic gunfire. Everyone else turned to witness the assault after hearing the gunshots. Sue vomited.

"Move!" Rob shouted at everyone to follow him past the front desk, out back to the swimming pool. As he held open the exit door, he called Major Calvert on his mobile.

"Major, we're under attack at the hotel!"

Rob wasn't able to explain further as a flying, quadcopter drone appeared outside the front doors next to the turnstile and shattered the glass with gunfire, striking him with a flesh wound just above his clavicle, fortunately missing his carotid artery but completely splattering the side of his face in blood. He dropped his phone amid the shattering glass and turned to join the others out back as the armed drone followed, continuing to fire shots through the glass doorway.

Sara led the group, her parents, Greg, Rob, Sue, Andrei and Danica to a side exit in the brick wall surrounding the pool, out onto the sidewalk and street. Rob was the last to join them.

Sue cried out upon seeing Rob's injury. "Rob, you're hurt!" She wiped the blood from his face before realizing it was from his shoulder.

"No time, Sue!" He pushed her hands down to her sides. "It's a drone! Hear it?" Everyone listened. "Everyone jump under a parked car! Two people per car! Fast!"

They rushed into the street and crouched down on the street side of the parked cars as couples, Sara pairing with Greg. They weren't fully under the cars before the drone hovered over them, but it didn't see them as apparently the camera was searching down the street.

The drone flew to the nearest corner and hovered. Seeing nothing, it darted down past them to the opposite corner and hovered there. Seeing nothing again, it returned to where they exited the gate in the brick wall, hovering above the street. It then lowered to the pavement and spied Rob. Sue was between him and the curb. He was grateful for that as he closed his eyes in expectation of the gunfire. He nearly lost control of his bowels as he heard the sound that followed and didn't see the delivery truck flatten the drone into the pavement.

He opened his eyes after hearing the crash. "Oh God."

***

Rob was the first to scoot back out from under the car and stand up, followed by Sue. "Everyone, it's fine. The drone's been smashed. You can come out."

One by one, with the men assisting the women, they stood back up and gathered around what was left of the drone, joined by the truck driver. They were startled by the drone-like sound of two approaching helicopters but quickly regained their composure as the choppers came into view over the buildings.

Sue noticed Rob wobble and led him to sit down on the curb. "Can someone call an ambulance?"

Sara made the call as she incidentally learned from something she read during her working visit that the equivalent of America's 911 in Europe is 112. Greg removed his shirt and pressed it against Rob's injury to staunch the blood flow. Soon, everyone pivoted from staring at the dead drone to gather around Rob.

Helicopters landed in the intersections at the two ends of the street and soldiers exited, taking crouched positions with machine guns. Calvert trotted up to the group surrounding Rob from one chopper and Fitzmaurice marched from the second, out of sight to survey the soldiers killed in their jeep in front of the hotel.

Wielding a pistol, Calvert shouted, "Where's the attacker?"

Sara pointed to the dead drone.

Calvert took a moment to process the scene and eventually holstered his weapon. "What happened? Where's Mr. Warner?"

The weary travelers parted to expose a view of Rob sitting in what was now a completely blood-soaked shirt.

"Have you called an ambulance?"

At the same time Sara responded, "Yes," Calvert yelled back to a soldier to bring first aid.

Calvert determined Sara, Greg and Andrei would be his best resources for a readout and barked at the three of them to follow him back into the hotel.

They walked around to the front of the hotel. Three soldiers were at the jeep with Fitzmaurice, who signaled Calvert to join them. Calvert instructed the others to wait for him inside the tattered lobby.

He rejoined them fifteen minutes later. Greg detected a lack of certainty about him, and a paleness to his face.

"Are you all right, Major?"

Calvert looked to Greg, squarely in the eyes, and nodded negatively.

"Were they your men?" Greg continued his concern.

"No. Fitzmaurice." Calvert sensed now that Greg was leading the conversation and knew he needed to take control.

"Okay, is there a conference room nearby where we can talk in private?"

Sara pointed to the side, "Down that hall."

Calvert replied, "Let's go."

He closed the door once inside. It was a convention size room that could seat over one hundred people, but there were only a dozen or so chairs and two tables randomly placed about. He assessed everyone with a direct look, engaging each of them with a quick glance in the eyes. He determined Sara appeared the least fazed and Andrei the most impacted. Andrei looked how Calvert felt. He started with him.

"Tell me what happened, Mr. Popov."

"We were all gathered in the lobby to see Sara off. Sara and I arrived here about twenty minutes earlier, from the Doughnut. She was just gathering her gear to join you for the flight home. The two soldiers were waiting outside in the jeep, parked where it is now. Then we heard gunfire and saw the soldiers being shot. It was the most gruesome thing I've ever seen Major."

"I can imagine. Go on."

"We ran to the back of the hotel, exited to the pool area and out the side gate to the street. Turned out the shooting was from a drone. It fired its way through the hotel after us and was on us before we could run anywhere. Our only option was to duck under parked cars. At first it didn't see us, but it figured things out and lowered itself to the pavement to search under the cars. Then bam! A delivery truck ran it over. Unbelievable."

"Why do you think the drone attacked you all?"

"I think it was after me, Major." Andrei looked at Greg and Sara as he said this. "I mean, after everything the GRU invested in the attack at Lake Ohrid, it seems plausible."

"I agree. We might learn something from tracing the gunpowder. Very unique tech, but forensics take time. Meanwhile, we'll operate under the assumption that Fancy Bear wants you dead Mr. Popov, and that Mr. Foyer and Miss Thomas here are not targets. Why was Mr. Warner shot?" Calvert looked to Greg to answer this question.

Greg responded, "He was holding the door open for us to escape. I'm not sure whether it was targeting him or just trying to shoot through the glass to enter the hotel."

"What did I tell you about Mr. Warner finding trouble?"

"Major, you can't seriously think?" Greg didn't feel like he needed to finish his sentence.

"No. Sorry. It's just." Calvert didn't finish his thought either.

"Miss Thomas."

"Sir."

"Come here." Calvert held out his arms and Sara embraced him, immediately melting into tears.

"Your parents can fly home with you on the military transport if you want them to. It's ready for you now. I won't be able to leave, but I understand you've been wanting to spend more time with your parents anyway."

This made Sara laugh. She broke from the hug and patted her wet face with her sleeve. "I hope you don't think I'm a big baby, Major. I can keep working with Andrei if you need me."

"I do have more work for you, Miss Thomas, but you can do it from Austin. Take the weekend off and report to your office on Monday."

"Yes, sir."

"I'll walk you out." Calvert looked back at Greg and Andrei and instructed them to remain in the room. He exited the room with his arm over Sara's shoulder.

***

Calvert returned to the conference room fifty-five minutes later. Not ones to be unproductive, Greg and Andrei were seated at a table eating a large breakfast.

"Sorry to keep you gentlemen waiting. I had a long conversation with little Sara's parents, as you can imagine. And I had to touch base with my commander."

"No worries Major," Greg said. "We got you a plate."

"Oh, well done Mr. Foyer. And coffee, thank God." Calvert seated himself and talked as he ate.

"Change of plans for you Mr. Popov. We have your asylum and British passports ready for you and Miss Ivanova, but you're traveling to Austin with little Sara. Be ready in sixty minutes. A jeep will pick you up outside the lobby.

"Mr. Foyer, you'll escort Mr. Popov and his companion. The Thomas family will host him and Miss Ivanova at their residence and he'll work from the Response Software offices. They'll start out in a hotel though. Apparently Sara's parents want to stay here for a few more days. God knows why.

"Mr. Popov, you're going dark. We figure you were spotted at the airbase in Ukraine and tracked here. We can't trust the military going forward. At least not in Europe."

Greg took advantage of Calvert's pause while pouring a second cup of coffee to begin asking questions.

"Did you see how Rob is doing?"

"No, sorry. Mr. Warner and Sue were already transported to the hospital before I returned outside. The Thomas's said he appeared fine though. I can have your escort stop by at the hospital if you men can be ready in thirty minutes."

"I appreciate that, Major." Greg continued. I've been tracking the fighting on my mobile. It appears over. I have to say, seems sort of fast?"

"Does it? Well, I think you know that Ukraine benefitted from some NATO assistance in areas. You also know that I can't discuss details with you. I will tell you that, regardless of media reports, we don't consider the hybrid component of this skirmish to be over yet. Hence, the need for you to establish Mr. Popov's readiness by 0600 CDT tomorrow morning."

"Yes, sir."

"And Mr. Popov?"

"Yes, Major."

"I spoke to Miss Ivanova outside. You're mother and brother are already on a flight to Austin. With British asylum and passports as well."

***

Andrei remained in the jeep while Greg visited Rob for a few minutes in the hospital. He entered Rob's curtained area in the emergency department to see Sue sitting there, holding his hand, with as much blood on her own shirt as he saw on Rob earlier on the sidewalk.

"Sue, you should go down to the gift shop and buy a clean t-shirt while I'm here. Someone might mistake you for a patient."

"Oh, that's sweet of you Greg. Thanks for coming by. I think I'll take you up on that." Sue left them.

"Rob, you on any medication?"

Rob was awake but slow to respond.

"No. Ibuprofen. I got some stitches, that's all."

"You seem a little down?"

"Yeah, I guess so. I'm still processing being shot. Doctor figures I got hit by two bullets. I just can't get over it, Greg. Sue could have been killed out there."

Rob was processing many things that left him melancholy. He was grateful for being athletic enough to shim under a car at his age. It occurred to him that athleticism can't out-run bullets. Mostly, he wished Sue never joined him on this trip. He understood his recklessness was incompatible with marriage, something he should have learned thirty years earlier.

Time to grow up. He often imagined himself in his prime whenever he worked out. If we was running, he recalled his college track races. Time to put immature thoughts like that behind him. Bullets change things.

"Rob, you didn't put Sue in harm's way. No one could have anticipated that."

"Yes Greg, I did put her in harm's way and I should have anticipated that. Actually, now that I think about it, Calvert should have. He should have protected us with guards."

"Sounds like you're moving from the self-loathing stage to anger."

Rob laughed at this. "Heh, yeah. Being mad feels better than depression. You have to agree with me Greg, I think you even said this back in Germany, there's no reason for me to be here. I should have returned home last weekend. I allowed this to happen by not going home."

"I won't argue with that. Calvert said something to me yesterday. He said this isn't just cybercrime. And that cyberwar will get you killed."

"Hmm. I should be released in the next hour. Sue booked us a direct flight to Denver on Norwegian Air for 2 pm. First class was the only thing available, but I feel like we might need it. Think the doctor would write me a prescription for first class?"

"You can ask. I'm leaving now myself with Andrei and Danica. Flying back to Austin on the military transport with Sara."

"What?"

"Calvert wants to get Andrei out of here. Too many Russians. He's even flying Andrei's family to Austin. He's taking every precaution going forward."

"Why are you traveling to Austin instead of Boulder?"

"He wants me to set up Andrei in our office there."

"What?"

"You had to figure Rob, it's just a matter of time before we're all working for Calvert."

"The news is saying this is over. Ukraine overtook the Separatists before sunrise."

"Yeah, that was impressive. I want to talk to Andrei more on the flight about the impact from his contributions. This was classic hybrid warfare, where you incapacitate the enemy ability to fight with a massive cyberattack before rolling in the tanks. Calvert is calling this Cyber War II."

"No doubt. He already talking to the media?"

"He was prepping for interviews when I left."

"Calvert's a piece of work. I'm not comfortable hosting Andrei in our Austin office. What's he going to be doing?"

"The Ukraine battle might be over, but this cyberwar isn't. I got the impression from Calvert that it's just starting. My orders are to have Andrei set up first thing in the morning."

"Then expect me down there by Monday."

***

"Sasha, I don't blame you. I'd like to, but our friends are going to hold me accountable. And rightfully so. At least we didn't lose our stash in the futures market."

General Volkov chuckled. Growing up with Putin, he understood his humor.

"You laugh Sasha, but that was important to our friends this morning. I offered to resign. You know what they said to me?"

"What did they say, sir?"

"They said to me, Mr. Putin, we still have Crimea. We're still ahead."

"Absolutely, sir."

"And with Nord Stream 2 fully contracted for the next two years after launch, Ukraine is less strategic to us now."

"Per plan, sir."

"Make no mistake, Ukraine is Russia. We will return to that

project soon enough. And you know Sasha, I don't think NATO cares that much about Ukraine."

"What do you mean, sir?"

"I don't think conquering the Separatists was their end game. Maybe for Ukraine, of course, but not for NATO. I think demonstrating their hybrid war capabilities was their objective. We've been demonstrating leadership in this domain, Estonia, Georgia, Notpetya, and they felt they owed us a response. Ukraine was simply the board for their game.

"We've lost Ukraine for now. I accept that. But we haven't lost this cyberwar. They think it's over. It's not."

"I understand, sir."

"I want a list of American assets to strike by end of day. I want critical infrastructure. Energy. Communications. Finance. I also want that Response Software firm wiped off the face of the fucking planet. And find Andrei."

"Understood, sir."

"I want Fancy Bear operating from within America in case they compartmentalize the Internet. We're taking this fight to their shores."

"I'm on it, sir."

***

"It's really nice of you to give us this ride to the airport, Major."

"It gives us a chance to talk, Mrs. Warner. And I like the certainty of seeing your husband board a plane."

"I suspect that's directed at Rob, Major."

"Indeed, Mrs. Warner. You must think we look a bit silly, both of us wearing our arms in a sling?"

"I'm tempted to take a photo, but I'm more worried about you two than humored."

"Fair enough. I know exactly how you feel. Mr. Warner, you're awfully quiet?"

"I should have asked for something a little stronger than ibuprofen. I do have questions though for you, Major."

"I have some muscle relaxers?"

"Hmm. No. I'd rather be able to drink on the flight. First class, you know."

"Ah, good call. What would you like to ask me?"

"I understand Andrei will be working in my Austin office?"

"Right. Actually Mr. Warner, I have assignments for a half

dozen of your people. Your perimeter will be guarded by my men for as long as I run operations there."

"Good, I was going to make that request. How long do you expect to run operations there?"

"I have to remain in Europe for the next two weeks. Upon my return, I'll relocate Andrei to my ops center in San Antonio."

"Why don't you start Andrei out there now?"

"There's no one there. They're all here."

"I see." Rob didn't have another question ready, but his tone suggested he was not finished.

"Mr. Warner. I'm sharing quite a bit of sensitive information with you. I hope you appreciate that?"

"I do Major, but you are commandeering my company."

"I am. You have some exceptional skills on your team that can assist Andrei in his efforts."

"Can you set my expectations around what those efforts entail?"

"I can at a high level. We're installing a satellite connection for your network so that Andrei and those working with him, namely Sara and Greg, and Sara's team lead, Jen - she's good - they'll have out-of-band access to the European Internet and our military network."

"In case you compartmentalize the Internet?"

"Exactly. But honestly Mr. Warner, there's a chance Andrei and your team might not do anything."

Rob gave the major an incredulous look.

"What I mean by that is they are positioned for counterstrikes. If Russia attacks us, they'll attack Russia. They have a list of targets and will attack from Austin."

"I guessed they'd be protecting America's critical infrastructure."

"I have teams on location all over the country. I even have the National Reserve deployed at critical sites. Lessons learned from last year's cyberattack at Mansfield Dam." Calvert and Rob exchanged a knowing look.

"Response Software will serve as my stealth ops center for offensive actions. Not truly counter-offensive, because they won't be defensive and will be asynchronous in terms of targets. Russia might punch us in finance, we'll respond to their energy sector. Really, whatever soft targets present themselves. Most bets are that Russia won't respond for months. I have to be prepared though. Once these attacks escalate, if they escalate, it's scary to imagine the potential outcome. This is a new kind of war."

"So this was never just a response to my team being attacked on the Norfolk Coast Path. Clearly, you had these war games planned ahead?"

"This was all about helping Ukraine take their country back and exercising our hybrid war capabilities. Including the war games. Somehow you stumbled into the middle of things. We didn't know about the wind farm breaches. I count Justin as our first civilian casualty of these hybrid war games. K.C. killed two Russians on that trail. And private Yankee was our first NATO casualty. At least five Russians and maybe a dozen Macedonian casualties in Lake Ohrid. I keep saying, Cyberwar will get you killed. That's why I'm here to see you board a plane, Mr. Warner."

"What's your feeling on how this might escalate, Major?"

"Communications we generally associate with Fancy Bear have gone dark the last couple of hours. They're certainly planning, if not mobilizing. I think Andrei is going to be busy."

Chapter Twelve

"YOU need to change that bandage and put on a clean t-shirt before coming to bed, mister."

"Geez Sue, is that any way to speak to a wounded vet?"

"Vet?"

"Yeah. I should be given a purple heart for being wounded in Calvert's cyberwar."

"I'd be happy if the Major reimbursed our deductible. Safe to say the U.K. will be out of network."

"Yeah, good point."

Rob was quiet for a few minutes, while he changed his bandage in the bathroom, then donned a fresh t-shirt and joined Sue in bed.

"Oh, feels good to be in our own bed, baby."

"It always does."

"You said Ella is coming tomorrow for brunch?"

"Yes. I thought we'd go to Lucile's. She likes their chicory coffee. She might spend the weekend too. You're not expected to join us for the OBGYN visit on Monday if that's going to be your next question."

"You know me well, Sue." Rob paused before he said, "I'm going to catch an afternoon flight to Austin tomorrow."

Sue sat back up and whacked Rob in the chest, forgetting about his injury.

"Are you dense, Rob? Calvert spent half the ride to the airport today advising you to stay clear of this thing."

"That's not what I heard him say."

"You are dense. You've been thrown off a cliff and shot, all in one week's time."

"In Europe. Calvert seemed to think Austin was safe enough for Andrei and my employees to continue his hybrid warfare. I can't allow for my staff to be subject to the whims of a clearly delusional major in U.S. Cyber Command, and not be there myself. What kind of employer would I be?"

"That sort of makes sense to me Rob, and I admire you for it, but what sort of confidence do you think you'll instill in your staff when they see you wearing your arm in a sling?"

Rob wasn't sure how to respond to that, then he caught the smirk on Sue's face. She was still hunched over him with her hand on his chest. Then she straddled him and started to kiss his face. Then his lips. She seemed to know when he was ready and made all the moves for her wounded warrior.

***

Rob gave Ella a strong hug, which she returned in force, after she walked into the house Saturday morning. He wasn't wearing his arm sling, to test out not wearing it in Austin. He was fine until Ella returned the strong hug. He won't hug anyone in Austin.

"You ready for Lucile's, sweetie?"

"God yes, I love that place."

"Ethan didn't want to join us?"

"He's practicing with his band all weekend. They have a show Thursday night. They're getting paid for this one."

"Oh, then he should practice,"

"Haha. Where's mom?"

"She'll be out in a second. I'm going to pull the car out of the garage. I'll be waiting outside. Tell mom to get going."

Rob expected Ella and Sue would begin talking and forget about him waiting outside. They typically did. He used the time in the car to call Greg.

"Rob?"

"Morning Greg. I'm flying down this afternoon. Will you guys still be at the office around 4:00?"

"Probably. Calvert know you're coming down here?"

"Jesus, Greg. I don't work for Calvert. Neither do you."

"Well, it sort of feels like I do this morning. I'm already in the office with Andrei. We had a planning call with Calvert and some other staff from the U.K."

"What did you talk about?"

"North American DNS servers are being DDoS'd this morning. Big one, like the Dyn attack last year. The telcos are collaborating on mitigation."

"So, we know it's Russia? This is their escalation?"

"Not much reason to DDoS the Internet on the weekend. We're assuming it's Russia and preparing a counterattack."

"Can you share details with me?"

"Yes, but not over the phone. We'll likely have started our response by the time you show up. Our offices are going to be ground zero for this, Rob."

Rob silently reaffirmed to himself that he needed to be in Austin to take responsibility for his staff.

"I'll ping you if my flight's delayed."

***

General Alexander Volkov went by Alexander Wolf on his fake German passport. Wolf means wolf in both German and English, as does Volkov in Russian. He considered a play on words for bear, but he started his fake passport collection before he earned the Fancy Bear moniker. He signed and went by his nickname Sasha when stealth traveling, it kept him more relaxed.

Sasha spent Friday night in Miami, arranging resources from a Russian Mafia group that was already set up for electronic payments from the GRU. Flights to New York, where the main leadership was located for this particular organization, were much cheaper, but he'd been to their offices there before and Miami was so much nicer.

Conducting transactions was professional and easy with these guys, he should have used organized crime for his recent wet ops in the U.K. It would leave his team to focus on their core operations, while avoiding international incidents when ops go bad. Live and learn.

Sasha checked into the Stephen F. Austin Hotel on Congress Avenue, Saturday at noon.

"Could I have a room with a view of the Capitol?"

"Let me check that for you, sir."

The front desk clerk was a middle-aged woman, regally poised, with a Texas drawl that spoke friendliness and hospitality to Sasha.

"We have the Governor's Suite available sir, with views of both the Capitol Building, and Lady Bird Lake to the south. But I'm afraid it's only available for the first week of your stay. We'd need to move you to another room after that."

Sasha thought about it. He knew it would be expensive, but he required both comfort and space to host his four operatives for strategy sessions. His delay in responding caused the clerk to prompt him.

"I can tell you, sir, there are also very fine views of the Capitol from the terrace at our tavern on the mezzanine."

"The Governor's suite sounds perfect. I may not actually be here for the entire two weeks."

"I'll add that note to your details, sir."

***

Sara woke up to her mom's ringtone. Seeing the time on her clock, 1 pm, *Oh it feels nice to be back in my own bed.*

"Hi, mom. You at the airport?"

"Your father and I decided to spend another week here, Tigger."

"Okay. You and dad have fun, mom." Sara was ready to hang up.

"You know how to take care of everything, right Tigger?"

"Yes mom, I'll be fine." Sara laid back down, suspecting this call might last a while. It did.

After hanging up, Sara recalled her mom telling her how they had to travel to the U.K. to be with her. And that she would understand when she became a parent. *How come they don't have to return with me?*

Still laying in bed, Sara messaged her best friend.

"Katie, I'm back."

"Tigger! Is that a British accent? Such a mimic."

"Stop. We're texting. I'm not talking British."

"r2."

"Breakfast at Maudies?"

"Lunch."

"Cya in 30."

The two Russians watched Sara drive off from inside their rental parked down the street. They were pleased to identify that the car she drove was a white, two-door Jeep with no roof.

***

Greg and Andrei were the only two people working inside the Response Software offices, located off Loop 360, if you didn't count the six soldiers guarding the perimeter from the parking lot and other more stealthy locations.

It wasn't unusual for a few staff to come in on Saturdays, but everyone was pretty well fried after working twelve hour days during the previous week for Major Calvert. Greg didn't learn about the extent of Calvert's commandeering of his company's staff until he returned and read some of their emails. After giving Andrei a tour of the offices, they sat on a couch in the lounge drinking expresso and discussed their targets for the coming week.

"On the one hand, Calvert's guidelines are pretty vague," said Greg. "Disrupt civilian life. Slow down the Russian Internet with persistent DDoS attacks. Essentially, make life hard."

"We can do that," responded Andrei.

"On the other hand," Greg continued, "Calvert asked us to come up with targeted attacks against Putin's cronies."

"I can't see us mounting an effective phishing attack, especially a spear phishing attack, in only one or two weeks. My bot army is going to be more useful for the DDoS attacks."

"Let's say we can somehow compromise Putin's top ranks. We have their profiles. That's step one. What could we do that would hurt them?"

"We steal their money. Go after their bank accounts. Their trading accounts."

"I read through the profiles Calvert gave us on the flight home. I didn't see any information on bank accounts." Greg felt like Andrei was onto something, they needed to talk this through.

"They all bank in Cyprus. And the Baltic countries. We hack those institutions and find their accounts."

"Hmm."

***

"Katie, you have no idea how wonderful coffee is. Take a sip. I can't believe my parents never told me about this."

Sara was sitting outside on the patio at Maudies with her best friend, eating a large plate of huevos rancheros.

"So, you're home alone?"

"I am, yeah, but my point is that my parents won't come back home to be with me here, like in Europe. If they trust me on my own now, that just proves my mom used me being in Europe to get dad to take her there."

"I got that the tenth time, Sara. What are you doing tonight?"

"I don't know." Sara looked up from her food to look at Katie.

She understood Katie's line of questioning once she saw her face. *Slumber party at my house.*

"There's not much food in our house," Sara said.

"I'll take care of that. You ever been to a Fresh Plus grocery? There's this cool little one in Hyde Park, around 43rd and Duval."

"That a new chain going after Whole Foods?"

"No, honey bunches. Fresh Plus was here decades before Whole Foods."

"You buying the groceries?"

"Absolutely, Tigger."

"Okay, let's go there next."

***

Sara, now Tigger, and Katie were pushing a cart down a box food aisle. The food cart was under-sized, as if to maintain an aesthetic with the dimensions of the store itself. Tigger and Katie flanked opposite sides of the cart, allowing no gap between themselves and the shelving for other shoppers to pass.

"Look at it this way Katie, little Miss Sunshine. My parents flew there, out of urgency to be with me, first class."

"Tigger, let them enjoy themselves. It was about you then. It's about them now."

"No. I can't. My mother is using me to get what she wants. I flew home in, what I can only describe, as a harness tethered to the inner web of a plane's outer shell."

Katie understood Sara because they'd been friends since toddler age. She knew Sara was describing the plane ride earnestly. She winced as a response.

"One of the military guys told me that he, and all his men, inserted catheters into their urethrae."

"Their what?"

"Urethrae. Plural for urethra."

"Urethra?"

"You don't know what an urethra is?"

"Did it fight Godzilla once?"

"It's where guys pee from, sweet Jesus, Miss Sunshine, are you that friggin' stupid? It's a flesh-tube or something that guys pee through. They stick this medical tube into their urethra, and they call that tube a catheter."

Katie made a disgusting face, with a hint of empathy.

"Do they lube it first?"

"You know Miss Sunshine, I didn't think to ask him that question?"

"Damn Tigger," said Katie. "You found yourself in some crazy shit this summer."

Both girls carried their laughs through the checkout and into the parking lot. They saw a guy get up, from what apparently was the ground, to a position standing between Sara's Jeep, and the other car parked on the driver's side.

Sara wanted to say something to him because she couldn't pretend he wasn't there. She was self-conscious of the adrenaline putting her senses into overdrive. Her next awareness was upon discovery of no one speaking for a spell.

"Drop something?"

"Yes."

Russian accent.

"My keys." The man, towering in size, smiled as he walked past, holding up his car keys.

The girls grabbed each other's hands as the man walked away. Sara scanned the cement near her car door for clues. All she saw was dirt, so she got in the car and didn't start talking until they both had their doors locked.

"Should I start up the car?"

Tigger needed the emotional support of Miss Sunshine at this moment to drive the car out of the garage. Miss Sunshine verbally directed her out to the street before their dialog turned to the man they both saw.

"He was Russian," said Sara.

"He was huge," Katie said. "I've watched enough Law and Order to know he's a bad guy."

"Why would he be picking up his keys on the passenger side of his car," Sara asked. "That doesn't make any sense."

"Yeah," replied Katie. "That's why it was weird."

"And because he was big. And Russian," added Sara.

***

After a half day of staring at LCD screens, Andrei and Greg agreed to reward their good progress by going out for barbecue. Greg planned to totally blow Andrei away by taking him up the road to an Austin barbecue landmark on the lake. Before they could open the doors to walk outside, the parking lot erupted in gunfire. The glass doors exploded from stray bullets and they dropped to the floor for protection.

The shooting lasted all of ten seconds, followed by shouting from the soldiers outside. Andrei and Greg didn't stand back up until several minutes later when a soldier came inside to check on them.

"You boys alright?"

"What the fuck, private?" Greg served in the military but never in a live combat situation.

The soldier responded, "Russian Mafia. Looks like a scouting mission. Hard for them to be coy though when no one else is driving around outside."

"So you just started shooting at them? How do you know they aren't employees?" Greg never expected an actual war at his office complex.

"We shot their tires when they tried driving away. They returned fire. They hit these windows here. Seriously, you guys okay? No one else in the building, right?"

"Just us." Greg looked at Andrei. "We're okay. Will police be arriving?"

"We'll handle that. You leaving?"

"We were going to head over to the County Line for lunch."

"Oh man, I heard about that place. Can you bring some ribs back?"

Greg looked at Andrei again. "Sure. I guess so."

"Oh, when you come back, expect to be stopped on Bridge Point Parkway before getting too close to the building. Change of protocol. Be sure to stop."

***

Greg and Andrei were on their second beer and just starting to eat, seated outside, close enough to the water to hear paddle boarders shouting at each other, before they began talking about the attack.

"Man Andrei, I felt like we were back at the Hotel Belvedere in Macedonia. How many days ago was that?"

"That was Wednesday night. Technically, Thursday morning. And you're forgetting we got shot at in the Westin Hotel in the U.K. yesterday. We've been shot at three days in a row now."

"Fuck."

"Yeah. This is the best barbecue I've ever had."

"Figured you'd like it. Remind me to place six orders for ribs when the waitress comes back by."

"Nothing from Rob?"

"No, he must be in the air. We'll hook up with him later back at the office. I'll text him to expect a military roadblock as he enters the office complex."

"You think he'll freak out?"

"Rob? No, I don't think so. He can roll with things pretty well. It's the rest of our staff. We need to decide if it's the right thing to do letting them come to work on Monday."

"What about us?" Andrei didn't look up from his food to talk. He moved on from his brisket to the ribs.

"Well, they can work from home, but we don't live here. I don't trust the hotel wifi. What's your place like?"

"It's a Residence Inn. But my entire family is there. I can't work there. But you know, my brother Josif could maybe help us. He's a gifted hacker. He could hack into those bank accounts."

"Would he do it?"

"In a heartbeat. Josif hates the fucking Russians."

Let's pick him up after lunch. I've spent all morning gathering vulnerability findings. He can get started with that."

***

Rob used to mostly read fiction when he flew. Now that he's running his own firm, his routine was to get online and work. He didn't have any work beyond email, but he was seriously behind on that since Sue joined him in Europe and tried to turn it into a holiday. He checked the Austin local news out of habit and saw an emerging story on a possible shooting near Bridge Point Parkway. He recognized that as the short drive off Loop 360 to his office building.

The article stated that Austin Police responded to reports of shots being fired in the office complex, and were met by the U.S. Cyber Command. The military set up a roadblock and wouldn't share any details with the police. *Brilliant. How many of my employees did Calvert get killed this time?* Rob was thinking of the employees of the Response Software firm, called Automated Responder at the time, before he became a partner a year earlier. He fired off an email to Greg, asking him if everyone was okay, then called him as soon as he landed.

Greg answered his phone, "Hey Rob. You here?"

"Just walking past the eateries by the gates. The Salt Lick smells tempting. We going out to eat tonight?"

"Sure.   Andrei and I already ate barbecue for lunch though. How about sushi? We haven't tried Sotos yet."

"Hmm, I wasn't thinking sushi but okay.   We could probably walk there. You staying at the Marriott downtown?"

"Yeah. I've got a car already so Uber over here."

"Sounds like a plan. I'll come over directly and check into the hotel later. Anything I should know?"

"Probably best to talk in person once you get here.   And don't try running any roadblocks."

"Okay. See you in a half hour."

Rob figured the roadblock quip was referencing the Cyber Command team that wouldn't share information with the Austin P.D. *A military roadblock in an office park. That has to look strange.*

Rob mulled over the events since Justin was killed in the U.K. as he rode in the backseat of the Uber.

Himself, K.C. and Justin were attacked by Russians after discovering a breach at an offshore wind farm. Presumably, because the CISO auctioned off their findings on the dark web.

Further discovery, confirmed by Calvert, suggested much of the European wind farm industry had been sabotaged by malware. Ostensibly an attempt by Russia to destabilize the clean energy market in Europe. The motive wasn't entirely clear, but energy is what drove Russia's economy.

Calvert was attacked, kidnapped actually, in their hotel in Macedonia. By Russians.

Meanwhile, NATO was performing war games in the Baltics, involving Calvert and implied a level of hybrid war was part of the exercises.

But was there a connection between the wind farm breach and the war games?

No. War games would take time to plan.

Then he, and everyone in his party, was attacked by a killer drone at the Westin in the U.K. Who was the actual target? Andrei maybe? Might have been stray bullets but it was himself who got shot.

This felt more like a Mafia drug war.

This started Rob to consider how today's cyberwar was perhaps an extension of the cold war. He wondered if it wouldn't be better if the US and Russia simply pulled the trigger on a good old fashioned conventional war. Upon arrival at the roadblock to his office building, he determined that whatever he was currently involved in, it wasn't cybercrime.

These are nation states fucking with each other.

Greg and Andrei greeted Rob in the lobby.

"At first I thought the glass to the front door looked incredibly clean. What happened to the door, Greg?"

"Russian Mafia shot it out. Andrei and I were standing right here. It was a little scary."

"Like in an actual battle with the U.S. Military?"

"Basically, yeah," Greg replied. "We suspect they were here to perform reconnaissance. Two of them. Being the weekend, they were sort of obvious. They probably didn't expect more than a security guard. It turned into a firefight. The Russians lost."

"Did you have to talk to the police?"

"Cyber Command handled it. We went to lunch."

Rob was struck by Greg's nonchalance. The apparent result of being in a war zone over the last few days. He noticed what looked to be a barbecue sauce stain on Andrei's t-shirt.

"Okay, so you two are here working on a Saturday. At the office. Except that, last time I checked, Andrei isn't employed here?" Rob finished this statement as a question.

"That's right, Rob," Greg explained. "Calvert has ordered us to spend the next week, maybe two weeks, launching cyberattacks against specific Russian targets. Primarily DDoS attacks against their critical infrastructure."

"He ordered you?"

"Well, tasked us. He said he could pay us if the expense is an issue."

"Just you two?"

"No. Andrei's little brother, Josif, is upstairs working on our plan to hack into some financials. And Calvert wants our entire office on this starting Monday. That's why he's assigned six soldiers to guard the place around the clock."

"Well then, he needs to write a damned check." Rob was incredulous. "Why do we need guards? No, forget I asked that. This is a problem. Russians were performing recon on our office building?"

"Russian Mafia per the CyberCom boys. Technically Americans," answered Greg. "I'm not sure we can put our employees into harm's way like this?"

"We absolutely cannot do that. I'll send an email this afternoon telling them the office is closed for the week and they can work from home. Do any of them know about this?"

"Not today's attack, as far as I know. But Calvert's already tasked at least Jen. He's had some of them working on this since last week. Not to mention little Sara. She was working with Andrei attacking Eastern Ukraine just the other day."

"Calvert's a piece of work."

***

Well before white settlers arrived in Austin, Native Americans enjoyed the spring at a site, now underwater, where the city's namesake, Stephen F. Austin desired to build a home on the property he then owned. He never did, but Clara Driscoll built a grand villa there during WWI, a place now well known as the Laguna Gloria Art Museum. Sara and Katie spent the afternoon there reviewing local contemporary art.

Sara was driving back to her house, with Katie in the passenger seat of her two-door Jeep, at the 35 mph speed limit through a commercial area that led to her neighborhood, when the accelerator suddenly pushed itself to the floor. In seconds, they were speeding at 65 mph. They flew through an intersection, narrowly avoiding a collision, as two cars bearing down on them from the sides somehow missed.

Katie screamed at Sara. "Sara! What are you doing?"

"I can't control it! The brakes don't work!"

Halfway through the next block, the jeep reached 85 mph and Sara had to steer into the oncoming lane to pass the car in front of her. Ahead was a T-intersection with a red traffic light. Sara downshifted into third gear, which slowed the car but she nearly lost control doing so. She was too scared after that to try second gear. The light turned green just as they sped through it.

The out-of-control vehicle entered the parking lot of a mattress store and was seconds away from crashing into a car parked in front of the store window when Sara yelled at Katie to jump out. Maybe a good plan but they were too late. They were both in a standing position on their seats, prepared to jump out, when they crashed into the parked car. The jeep flipped forward and ejected the two girls through the store's plate glass window at 70 mph. The jeep came to a rest halfway through the broken window.

The girls bounced across mattress pad displays from the front of the store to the back, with customers narrowly moving out of their way. Sara came to rest on a child's bed display against the back wall of the store, decorated with stuffed animals. A stuffed, Winnie the

Pooh, Tigger animal fell into her lap, causing Katie to burst out laughing.

Sara looked over at Katie, relieved to know they were both okay. Then she saw the blood gushing out of a gash on Katie's leg.

"Katie, we need an ambulance." She pulled her phone from her back pocket and dialed 911.

***

The General received two of the four Russian Mafia in the Stephen F. Austin hotel bar, outside on the mezzanine overlooking the Capitol building. Because the weather was uncomfortably hot, they were the only guests sitting outdoors and had the privacy needed to discuss business, as long as they weren't too loud. The street noise below offered further security, probably moot since they spoke entirely in Russian.

"When was the last time you spoke to your partners?" The General was referring to the other two men that comprised this four-man team from Miami.

One man did all the talking and the other remained silent.

"Just before noon. We all left a coffee shop at the same time. They left to scout the Response Software offices while we went to the home of their employee, Sara Thomas. The plan was to meet back up here."

"They don't answer their phones when I call them." This was another question the way the General stated it.

The same man responded, "I haven't tried. I will now."

He called both men without success.

"Keep trying. If they miss this meeting, have them join us for dinner at 7 pm at Soto Sushi. It's nearby. I've made reservations for the five of us."

"Yes, sir."

"Tell me about your operation."

The man couldn't answer immediately as a cocktail waitress interrupted them for drink orders. The General ordered a bottle of Deep Eddy Vodka, which, depending on how big of drinkers these two men were, he expected to be able to take up to his room. He had a shot earlier in the bar and found the brand to be okay. It was distilled ten times, which he figured was perhaps a necessity having been distilled from corn. He ordered it for the American experience.

The man responded after the waitress left.

"We successfully hacked the girl's jeep and caused her to crash into a building. She and her passenger were ejected from the vehicle, through a plate glass window and into a store. We saw her leave in an ambulance, so she's still alive, but we don't expect her to be working for a while."

"Good job, gentlemen. We don't necessarily need her dead. Just out of operation so she's no longer contributing to Andrei's efforts."

After the vodka and shot glasses arrived, the General led the men in planning attacks on Rob, Andrei and Greg, the only others he had recent intelligence on. He'd wait to hear back from the two other Mafia men at dinner to plan further attacks on the employees of Response Software. He instructed the men to leave their weapons in his hotel room while they enjoyed themselves at dinner.

***

After working throughout the afternoon, Rob, Greg, Andrei and his younger brother Josif walked from the Marriott to the Soto sushi bar on South Lamar. Andrei felt a bit guilty leaving his mom and girlfriend back at their hotel, but this was work. Turned out to be a good thing.

From their seats at the sushi bar, and as Rob paid the bill, Andrei recognized the General as he entered the restaurant with two very large men. The General saw him at the same time. It was a small space.

Andrei and the General launched into each other. The mafia men followed suit, attacking Greg and Josif, who tried their best to defend themselves. Rob was last to enter the fray. The punches lasted all of five seconds, leaving Rob, Greg, Andrei and his brother all on the floor. One of the mafia men gave Rob a final kick in his abdomen wound before fleeing with the General out of the restaurant.

The hostess called the police. One of the sushi chefs stepped out from behind the bar with a huge knife. The fighting was over though. Rob remained in a fetal position while the other three sat up, although still on the floor around Rob. No one said anything for a few moments until Greg noticed Rob was bleeding through his shirt.

"That doesn't look good, Rob."

"I think my stitches are torn. Hurts like hell."

"I'll call EMT." Greg dialed 911 on his mobile.

Andrei fussed over Josif, speaking to him in Macedonian. He was fine. The two of them had been in fist fights before. They'd yet to ever come out as winners. Hackers don't make great street fighters.

"What the hell just happened to us?" asked Rob.

Andrei answered, "That was Fancy Bear. The older guy."

Rob couldn't believe it. "That was the GRU? Here? In Austin?"

"Yep."

Rob looked to Greg. "Call Calvert. Wake the bastard up if he's still in the U.K."

"Calling now." Greg stood up and walked to a quieter space in the restaurant to hear better.

The other three stood up, with both Andrei and Josif helping Rob to his feet.

Rob asked if anyone got in a good punch. Andrei responded, "No, I swung first at the General but missed. God, that was embarrassing."

Rob said, "We need to start working out with K.C."

"Who's K.C.?"

"Calvert's wife. She's a bad-ass. She works with us. You'll probably meet her before this is over."

"I've never been able to fight," responded Andrei. "Probably a good thing I didn't hit anyone. Might have bruised my hands. Gonna need them healthy for the keyboard."

They all laughed at that. The police arrived and took their statements. Greg had the officers talk to Calvert over his phone, which helped to keep the questions short. The EMT arrived and treated Rob's torn stitches outside, avoiding a hospital trip. An hour later, they were back at the Marriott lounge drinking whiskey. With his bruised face, Josif didn't get carded.

Sitting on two over-stuffed leather chairs and a couch, Rob turned the discussion to planning their next steps.

"I don't think we should meet at the office tomorrow. You think you could join Greg and me here at the hotel tomorrow, Andrei? I'll book us a conference room."

"Sure, I could do that."

Greg interjected, "Calvert wants you to return home Rob. ASAP."

"Why?"

"For your safety. It's clear to him that Fancy Bear is targeting

Response Software. This little cyberwar has turned decidedly real."

"Yeah, I guess I would have to agree with you on that. I really can't believe that son of a bitch Fancy Bear traveled all the way here to attack us," Rob said.

Andrei responded, "I'm not surprised. The General is very much a hands-on kind of leader. He's visited me in person several times to give me direct orders."

Rob kept his questions directed to Greg. "What else did Calvert say?"

"He told me to check up on little Sara. I'll give her a call now. He's assigning troops to be our drivers and to guard us twenty-four seven from here on out."

"Okay, I don't mind going back home. Consider me off this thing. You need to be in Boulder yourself Friday, to close our transaction with CBI."

"Geez, I almost forgot about all that. Bill tell you the final number?"

"One hundred and fifty-five million." Rob couldn't help hold back a huge smile. "We've generated some press for ourselves the last couple of days. Bill leveraged that goodwill for another twenty million."

"Bill's good at what he does."

"Indeed. We've also got Justin's service the next day. It'll be up in Estes Park."

"That'll be a nice setting."

"Yeah. If the situation presents itself, we'll provide Justin's wife with a check for his shares."

"She expecting it?"

"Yes, but she has no idea of the size."

"Hope we survive another week to be presented with a check ourselves."

"Yeah."

Rob raised his glass to toast, "Here's to surviving one more week."

The men clinked their whiskey glasses, and Greg dialed Sara on his mobile. After saying hello, he was silent for a good couple of minutes. The three others watched him with interest as Sara was obviously relaying a great deal of information to him.

"So you girls are okay?"

Greg shared instructions that a military escort would drive her to the hotel instead of the office on Monday. This was all they heard from Greg until he said goodbye and hung up.

Rob asked, "What happened?"

Greg responded, "Sara's jeep was hacked into and remotely controlled. She and her girlfriend were nearly killed. They both got stitches in the hospital but are otherwise okay. She's staying at her girlfriend's parents' house now until her own parents return home from their trip."

"My God," said Rob.

"I'm going to have to share that with Calvert too. We're clearly under assault."

"Why? I don't get it."

Andrei suggested, "For the same reason the General is after me. The GRU doesn't let their enemies walk away."

"Well, Fancy Bear is on our turf now," Rob said.

Greg added, "Oh, that was another thing Calvert said. He said it was a mistake for Fancy Bear to come here."

***

The General reconvened with his two partners back out on the terrace of his hotel bar. Much more pleasant at night and again, all other patrons were drinking inside in the comfort of air conditioning. The bar terrace on Congress Avenue had become his war room. While he felt that perhaps his battle plans were off track, the bar fight had created a sense of camaraderie between him and his two partners. It felt good to him to be in the field.

"Where the fuck are the other guys?"

The more talkative partner responded, "I've got a local news item on my phone here about shots being fired this morning at the Response Software offices."

"Ah," the General sighed. "Idiots."

The General continued with battle plans.

"Okay, let's assume it's just the three of us now. I want you to continue here in Austin. Keep a safe perimeter around their offices, but close enough to track known targets driving in and out. Especially Andrei. If all you accomplish is killing Andrei, that's success. And to be very clear, he's no Sara. He dies. I need his murder to serve as a signal. It needs to be painfully slow and gruesome. Apparently his little brother is with him. Have Andrei watch as you kill him first."

"Understood, sir."

The partner who rarely spoke joined in with, "We should have killed them at the bar."

"No," the General corrected him. "There were cameras everywhere in that place. Although maybe we should have lingered outside to trail him home. Too late now and second-guessing ourselves serves little purpose. We learned who are working together. And that all of them are here in Austin. That's valuable intel. Retreating to plan our next steps was wise."

"This news alert says the military set up a roadblock to the entrance of the office park. We can't park on the highway, too visible. We'll have to hike in through the woods."

The General agreed with a nod. "Wait until Monday, when the place is full of other workers. Maybe you can get close enough to tag their cars with GPS."

"We don't have that kind of gear with us."

"Just duct tape one of your phones underneath the car."

"Hmm. That'll work."

***

Rob looked at his face in his hotel bathroom mirror. He had a new bruise on his chin. He hadn't been in a fist fight since grade school. Then he remembered he was just in a fist fight a week earlier when he got punched and kicked over a cliff. And then he was shot by a God damned drone of all things. *Christ. What am I doing?*

The two whiskeys had him feeling a bit drunk. He was used to beer. He knew he should call Sue. Instead, he sent her a text to pick him up at noon Sunday from the airport. He'll tell her everything but not until he's home. He didn't need her worrying about him.

He didn't sleep well. He was not normally introspective, but he thought about his future. Six days from now, Sue and he will be wealthy. He hadn't figured out the taxes yet, but their net worth will be in the twenty million range.

In the last week, he could have been killed twice. Three times if he counted Macedonia. And Sue could have been killed with him. It was clear to him that he needed to let this go. *This is a cyberwar and war is for soldiers. Introspection is good.*

***

Sunday morning, Rob joined the others for breakfast before heading to the airport. Since they had a military driver, they left the hotel for Kerbey Lane, which Rob considered the best breakfast in

145

Austin.

Greg informed Rob of his plans for the week.

"I thought about it last night and there's really no benefit in going to the office. We'll be working through proxy servers, so our bandwidth will suck no matter where we are."

"Good point," replied Rob. "I already booked you a conference room at the hotel for the week. You might want to pick up some computers though."

"Oh yeah, good thinking. We'll want some big monitors too. We can go to Fry's today.

"I let Calvert know and he said he'll continue to guard the office park. It might serve as a honeypot for Fancy Bear."

"Tell Sara to take the week off. Paid vacation."

"We're going need her, Rob. We're going to need everyone," countered Greg. "This is all hands on deck. Calvert gave us a year's worth of targets to DoS."

Rob wasn't comfortable with this. "What can she do? Sara's not a hacker."

Andrei interjected, "Au contraire. She is after working with me Thursday night. I've never seen such a fast learner. What's that girl's IQ?"

Greg was happy for Andrei's support. "Yeah, Sara has some special skills. I was thinking she could work with Josif to hack the financials. We'll have a driver bring her down here each day to work in the same room with us."

Rob checked himself. "Okay. I'm not going to tell you guys what to do. I'm backing away from all this. Just be safe."

"Safety first, Rob."

The men, all sporting bruised faces, nodded collectively in confirmation.

***

The General enjoyed the bar terrace one more time, for breakfast. He intended to check out afterward. He knew he needed to leave Austin after the previous day's visibility. The odds of his mafia partners being captured were high and he needed separation. And his updated intel on Rob provided him with his flight itinerary. Rob was returning to Boulder this morning. He booked himself a later flight using yet another identity.

Chapter Thirteen

Sue collected Rob outside the baggage terminal at DIA.

"Hey there, sailor. Need a ride?"

"If it's not too much trouble, ma'am."

"Not at all. Hop in."

Rob threw his bag in the back seat before sitting down. He liked it when Sue flirted like this. He imagined himself in a sailor suit, kissing her wearing a nurse outfit, like in the famous Times Square photo by Life Magazine. He kept this thought to himself.

"Did you eat? I thought we could go to the Med for lunch. Maybe an early supper. There's not much food at home."

"I could do that," answered Rob.

"Oh darling, what's on your face?"

"Bit of a bruise."

"What happened?"

"I got into a sushi bar fight last night."

Rob thought his play on words was funny but Sue missed it.

"A fight? You're a fifty-five-year-old man! Grown men don't get into bar fights."

"They did last night. Greg, Andrei and I, and Andrei's little brother too, were attacked by some Russians after dinner."

"What?"

"Let me explain."

"Please."

"The Russians followed us to Austin. The guy who runs the GRU, Russia's military intelligence, a General Alexander Volkov, and two other men who are apparently Russian mobsters but American. We think it was just by accident that they walked into the same restaurant we chose for dinner, just as we were leaving. The General and Andrei know each other, so as soon as they recognized one another, they launched into each other like two charging elk bucks."

"And you?"

"We all entered the fray like the benches clearing in a baseball game brawl. Seriously, the fight lasted only seconds. I got hit once and hit the floor. The Russians scrambled out of there as fast as they could."

"Well, why were they in Austin?"

"We think to attack our offices. I mean, really, it's hard to imagine what their motives were, but safe to say things have escalated."

"Should we be scared?"

"Well, I left Austin. I thought we could head up to the cabin tonight. Maybe go home after lunch and pack. It'll be our first night up there. We can spend the week hiking. I'll drive down Friday to close the transaction at CBI and come back up, since Justin's service is just a few miles down the road from the cabin."

"I like that plan. I'll ask Marty to show my houses for me. I don't need to work anymore."

"No. Neither of us does."

***

The General landed at DIA two hours after Rob. He already knew where Rob lived. Gleaned entirely from public sources, from LinkedIn to online Boulder County real estate records, his intel was highly detailed. He'd perform recon today and plan on how to best attack. He checked into the airport Westin. Not very close to Boulder but it would be convenient for his departure. He then rented a car and drove out to scout Rob's house.

The General was parked in his rental just down the street from Rob's house for less than twenty minutes when he spotted both Rob and Sue get into their car with a couple of overnight bags and a cooler on wheels. His first thought was to break into their house to gain familiarity and to leave a window unlocked for later. But then the fact they were carrying bags registered in his brain and he made the decision to follow them.

They had already turned a corner out of sight, but he found

them before they got too far away. Keeping his distance, he followed them up into the mountains. After almost an hour, they entered a dirt road. He was able to spot them parking at a cabin within sight of where he stopped on the side of the highway. His Boulder County records search didn't show him Larimer County real estate, and both Rob and Sue had their Facebook profiles locked down fairly tight.

He took some quick photos to be able to quickly find the location again, and continued driving on to Estes Park, a few more miles up the road where he checked into yet another hotel. He used credentials with his name, Alexander Volkov. He wanted CyberCom to know it was him.

***

Knowing she was going to a nice hotel downtown, Sara dressed as she imagined sophisticated women dress. A simple cotton dress, because she's Texan, but with jewelry and heels. Plus a light cardigan, despite the ninety-degree weather, because hotels can be cold inside. And the sleeves would cover the stitches she got on her upper arm from the crash.

After meeting Josif, and learning she'd be working with him all day, all week in fact, she was pleased with her fashion choice. The boy, two years older than her, was dreamy. She'd have to shop for more dresses downtown, before returning home today.

Josif explained the list of targets to Sara and how to map their known vulnerabilities to exploits. Sara was hacking as fast as Josif was explaining. Midway through the morning they were also engaged in flirtatious, albeit inane conversation. It didn't feel like work to Sara.

Trying to sound like she'd been to Europe before, Sara asked, "Isn't Macedonia really part of Greece? Or no, aren't they trying to get your country to change its name?"

"Uh, those towels? They can have their name. We would never want to be Latin. We're Slavic."

"Towels?"

"What you call gays."

"You think Greeks are Latin?"

"Yeah, all the men can dance. That's how you know they are Latin towels."

"I think the Romans were Latin. The Greeks are, are Greek."

"Greco Roman. All the men can dance."

149

"You can't dance?"

"I can dance. But you don't see me dancing all the time. That's the difference."

Sara couldn't hold her seriousness longer. She nearly fell out of her chair laughing.

Josif sensed she was laughing at him. She looked so pretty laughing though, he didn't mind.

***

The two Russian-Americans had spent Sunday studying online maps of the terrain they planned to hike Monday, and buying the right gear. Upon discovering how bad the early morning traffic was, they took a long breakfast and began their hike in from a pullout on City Park Road. The terrain wasn't difficult, but the heat and humidity were oppressive. They hiked up to the office complex slowly to avoid making noise and to look for soldiers along the way.

They found them, guarding the perimeter. The soldiers weren't necessarily hiding, but it wasn't possible to pass them to reach parked cars. That wasn't a problem because they could see from the woods that there weren't any cars parked in the lot. They maintained their spying for two hours in the event these hacker types arrived to work late. Eventually they returned to their hotel.

***

Volkov drove up to Rob's cabin early in the morning, parking down the road just out of site. He walked through the woods to where he could view the grounds. His plan was to perform recon on day one. It might seem like he was winging it by chasing Rob around, but his tactics followed a field ops checklist he'd learned over decades.

He was surprised to find their car gone. He knew about Rob's hiking hobby and figured it made sense they might have gone out early. It was also possible that just one of them left to get groceries while the other was still in the cabin. He spent thirty minutes walking a wide perimeter around the cabin. Recon 101.

The General wished he had a firearm. Having seen Rob fight two days prior, he was confident he could quite easily kill him with his bare hands, but there were two of them. The hunting knife he purchased Sunday in Estes Park while shopping for outdoor gear would have to do.

He determined from his reconnaissance that the cabin was too small for him to try to hide inside and wait to kill them there. The trail likely offered just as much privacy. But then, they might have the opportunity to run. They are no doubt in good shape and of course, they are acclimated to the altitude. The General was breathing heavy from his simple walk around the cabin.

Small or not, attacking the cabin would mitigate Rob's chance to escape. He spent the day waiting inside his car, with an ample supply of energy bars and water.

Rob and Sue returned to the cabin at 3 pm. That suggested perhaps Tuesday would be a similar routine. What he didn't yet know is when they would get up to leave in the morning, although he could guess it would be around sunrise based on today. He drove back to town to make plans for his Tuesday attack, debating on the optimal time of day.

***

By late afternoon, Sara and Josif had hacked into most of their targets. All oligarchs known to be close to Putin, many of them members of the Duma. They couldn't find traces of Putin's money, and a handful of their targets used two-factor authentication, which was effective against the methods they used to breach the accounts. Still, they gained access to nineteen targets and thirty separate accounts containing over two hundred billion dollars.

Josif said to Sara, "Let's call it a day. We're not going to get much more than this. Tomorrow we can begin designing how and where to move the money."

"Sounds good. How did you learn so much about international banking and financial systems, Josif?"

"Practice."

"I see." Sara asked, "How did you learn English? You take English in school?"

"No. I could, but I learn other ways better."

"Like how?"

"Western music. I always listen to rock and roll. My whole life. And many online chat is in English. I learn from that."

"Hmm. Say a lot of online chat."

"Why?"

"Instead of many online chat, say a lot of online chat. It's not the best English either, but it's what people would say colloquially."

"So say the word, alotof?"

"Right. Phrase actually. It's three words."

"A lot of."

"That's very good, Josif."

"As in, there are a lot of towels in Greece, no?"

"Oh, here we go again."

"Really Sara. You would not like Greeks. Greeks are, how you say of your president, misogynists."

"Impressive word, Josif. I bet it's Latin."

Josif caught the joke, but his wit wasn't fast enough in English to respond before she did again.

"You're saying Greeks are both towels and misogynists? I don't suppose those are mutually exclusive terms, but seems like a bit of a stretch."

"It's true. Latin women are very sexy. And Latin men want to be sexy too. You see how they like to dance. Latin men struggle with Latin women for control of the X chromosome."

"Do they teach you this stuff at school in Macedonia?"

"No. I learn this from the Internet."

"Oh, Josif. Sugarbunches. We're going to the bookstore after work. We're going to get you real books to read."

"Okay. Let's go now."

***

As Rob opened his cabin door to place their hiking boots outside on the porch, he heard a car engine start. He watched as the car that was parked along the side of the dirt county road, turned around and drove back to the highway. He wouldn't put much thought into it normally, but he purposely did now, all things considered.

There was no trailhead, indeed, there was no trail, near where the car was parked. It wasn't there in the morning when Sue and he left to hike in the Wild Basin park area. And he didn't see anyone as they drove in, yet the car was leaving only a few minutes after they returned to the cabin. The driver wasn't on the road or he would have seen him. Or her. So they must have either been in the car already and he didn't notice. Or they were in the woods although there are no trails. Odd.

Sue was sitting in one of the two leather chairs with a beer for herself and another one on the table for Rob. He asked, "You notice the car parked down the road as we drove in?"

"Yeah. Some sort of Jeep. I think the Patriot model. Really clean."

"You have a good eye, Sue."

"I've been looking at Jeeps lately."

"Hmm. Well, the owner just drove off. Did you notice anyone sitting in the car as we drove past it?"

"There wasn't anyone in the car. Unless they were lying down."

"We didn't pass anyone walking on the road either."

"Why are you so suspicious?"

"I think we have to be right now."

"Okay. Well, what can we do about it?"

"I don't know. Let's think about it."

***

The mafia men watched the local news in their hotel room as they discussed plans for finding Andrei. They were stunned when a video clip played of their Saturday night fight in the sushi bar. High-resolution images were shown for both them and the General. They would have to keep a low profile going forward, ordering delivery food. This was beginning to feel like work.

It was seeing a related video clip of the military that prompted one of them to consider their best option might be to follow soldiers as they left the office park. *They must be sleeping somewhere. Maybe Cybercom would lead them to Andrei.*

They drove back to the office park and picked a spot off the highway near the intersection of Loop 360 and Ranch Road 2222. They didn't have to wait long before they observed a military jeep driving away from the office park toward the center of Austin on 2222. They followed it.

This took them to Camp Mabry, a military base in the heart of Austin off West 35th Street. They parked on the side of the road and waited, discussing their next steps.

"I don't care about the General, we're not attacking a military base."

"Nope."

"Maybe we'll get lucky and see Andrei drive by?"

"Yep."

They waited. They noticed the pattern of jeeps leaving the compound and entering MoPac, the highway next to the base, and driving north, back toward 2222. Just before 5 pm, one finally broke this pattern and drove south on MoPac. They decided to follow it. Their luck panned out as it parked in front of a downtown hotel and Sara and Josif walked up and got inside. They followed it to a Barnes & Noble bookstore in the Arboretum.

***

Sara didn't instruct Josif on what to buy. They both browsed the bookstore according to their interests and met up after forty-five minutes.

"Just one book, Josif?" asked Sara.

"Well yeah, I can only read one book at a time." Josif took note of Sara's basket full of paperbacks. "That looks like an entire year's worth of books."

"I read a book a day." Sara was used to people's reactions. "I'm a fast reader."

"Wow. What do you read?"

"Historical fiction lately. I go through genres. I went through a dystopian phase in middle school. Women biographies and memoirs my freshmen year. Last year I read all thrillers."

"No romance books?"

"I went through that phase in grade school, along with fantasy."

"Wow. I've never known someone to read so much."

"It's what my family does. We sit around the house and read. My dad's a professor and my mom's a writer."

"Oh, that's cool. What kind of books."

"It's hard to describe. Sort of romance slash steampunk. She's good. I read all her books."

Josif didn't respond immediately. He caught himself thinking about meeting Sara's parents at her house. "Ready to check out?"

"Sure."

They ate dinner together at a restaurant in the Arboretum and meandered around the outdoor mall afterward. Josif took hold of her hand as they walked. Sara wasn't sure if this was just something Europeans do, or if he was crushing on her. She knew she liked it.

The soldiers dropped Sara off at her house before dark, as her parents were now home, before driving Josif to his Residence Inn hotel. The mafia men followed and waited in the parking lot after the military jeep drove off.

***

After working a long day, Greg and Andrei had drinks in the hotel bar and stayed there for dinner as well. They weren't taking chances.

"Andrei, I'm really impressed with your little brother. Sara too. I mean, they accomplished a year's worth of breaches in a single day. Is Josif some sort of genius?"

"He is pretty bright. Smarter than me, but he already had access to a lot of those financial firms. I think he had a lot of fun today. This gave him a reason to finally breach accounts."

"So he's had access to the systems, but never stole anything before?"

"Stealing money from trading firms is not as easy as you see in the movies. Most money is invested in equities. You have to sell the stock first. Sometimes, depending on what level of borrowing authority the target has, you have to wait a few days for the trades to settle before you can transfer the funds.

"You also have to disable email or text notifications, or change them to your own email. This is impossible to do with accounts that have two-factor authentication set up. While two-factor is inconvenient for account holders, it's becoming more and more pervasive.

"Then, you have to move the money to another account. It's not really possible to do that undetected and without leaving a trail. The best you can do is transfer the funds to another country that will be uncooperative with the target's home country. And use multiple personas. So you can slow down an investigation. But if it takes years for the U.S. Government to track you down, they will spend the resources and eventually track you down.

"So eventually, you have to remove the money from the financial systems. You have to buy gold or diamonds. Something like that. I deal with virtual currencies of course, but even that can be traced. Ultimately, you have to get your money offline."

"What is Josif's plan then for tomorrow?"

"He doesn't have one. He asked me to discuss a plan with you tonight."

"Hmm, okay. Well, he doesn't have to really ever take the money offline. Calvert said we should be prepared to eventually return the funds. The idea is to use the money as leverage to gain concessions from the Russians, then give it back. With that said, maybe all he needs to do is keep moving it around."

"Brilliant. He could definitely do that. That could even be automated if we need to do it for an extended period of time."

"Oh, nice. You could start coding that routine tomorrow while I keep working on the DDoS attacks."

"Sounds like a plan."

Greg remained at the hotel after dinner while Andrei returned to the Courtyard with his military escort. It was dark by the time they dropped him off.

***

Rob figured not having cell coverage or Internet at his cabin would be one of the benefits, until now. With everything that was going on down in Austin, and with his paranoia that the Russians might have followed him to his cabin, he felt exposed. And while he usually avoided disclosing possible dangers to Sue, this time he shared his concerns with her. If they were at risk, they would need to act as a team.

"Okay, with furniture against both the front and back doors, the Russians won't be able to enter the cabin without making some noise. Our jackets and boots are by the bed so we can make a quick escape out of whichever door isn't being broken into. We both have kitchen knives and this pot of water will be fairly hot resting on the wood stove. So we have a barricade for defense, weapons if we need to fight and gear ready if we choose flight."

"All those years as a boy scout are really paying off now, Rob."

Sue wasn't as worried as Rob and was able to find humor in their situation. Rob's been thrown off a cliff, shot by a drone, and beaten up in a sushi bar.

"Never hurts to be prepared."

"Well, now that we are, why don't you sit down with me and have a beer? The soup is ready too if you're hungry yet."

"I'm starving. I'll have a bowl now."

Rob joined Sue in their two leather chairs with his soup and beer. She was reading a large hardcover.

"I should have brought something to read too. We packed so quickly coming up here."

"We should bring Blake's stereo up here to play CDs. I don't think he's ever going to use it again. Music would be nice."

Mentioning their son made Rob think of his daughter.

"Ella doing okay with everything?"

"As well as can be expected. That Ethan went to her appointment with her today, and that she wanted him to go over me - that's a good sign their relationship is strong. I just wish I had a signal up here to call her today."

"Yeah, tell me about it."

"We'd have all the conveniences if we retire in Telluride. Have you been thinking more about that?"

"Baby, that's all I think about. In four more days, we'll be able to buy a home in every ski resort in the state. The closer we get to Friday though, the more acutely aware I become of the need to survive."

Rob drank down half his beer, which Sue poured into a pilsner glass for him.

"I tried to do the right thing by going to Austin to manage the welfare of my employees, but I chickened out and came home. I'm embarrassed to say it, but I'm in pure preservation mode."

"You've been through an awful lot lately, Rob. Your future isn't what you imagined a year ago. You're doing the right thing."

"I appreciate you saying that sweetie. I just don't know. To say that money is the most important thing doesn't feel right."

"It's not the money, Rob. It's your retirement. It's our welfare."

Sue rose from her chair to sit in Rob's lap. She caressed his cheek.

"We're entering a new chapter in our lives Rob, and it's going to be wonderful. Soon we'll have grandchildren. You'll take them hiking. That Major Calvert would have you fighting in his little cyberwar like you're a soldier. You're not a soldier, Rob."

"I know, you're right. He's coopted my firm like it's his own cyber platoon. I can't believe his actions are even close to being legal. I don't know why I let him do it."

"Because you enjoy it, Rob. You're a thrill seeker. That's why you climb fourteeners. But it's time for you to consider your age. Know your limits, Rob."

"Hmm, yep. These last couple of weeks have been nothing if not a constant reminder of my limits. When it's fight or flight, I'm a runner."

"That's right. Let's go to bed, darling."

"It's still early."

"I packed that drindl."

***

Andrei walked through the Residence Inn lobby before heading out the back door to his unit, to see if any chocolate chip cookies were left. There weren't any.

He didn't notice the two men follow him to the door. They rushed the door as he closed it, knocking him down to the carpet.

He rolled over and looked up at them, both pointing handguns at him. For a split second he detected the red laser dots on their foreheads before each of the men was shot twice and dropped dead to the floor, almost on top of him.

Andrei's unit was actually next door, which he entered through a double door from this unit. Cybercom was stationed in this apartment, with the lights off, guarding his family. Smart plan. There would be no interrogations though.

The men's identification and license plate provided Cybercom with enough intel to determine they were connected to the men they killed Saturday, that they drove from Florida, and that they have Russian Mafia history. What they didn't know was if there were still others in Austin undetected. Calvert instructed them to maintain vigilance after they called him with their operational status report.

***

Like Calvert, Volkov also expected a regular status report from what was left of his Austin team. When it didn't come, he suspected the worst. He moved his plan up from late Tuesday afternoon when he expected Rob and Sue to return from hiking, to early morning before they left the cabin.

He remained awake the entire night, partly from anxiousness, but there was also that much planning to do. Not just for the attack, but for his escape out of the country. He was tired at 4 am when he drove back to Rob's cabin, and he wondered if it would have been wise to catch at least a couple of hours sleep.

Volkov parked his car down on the highway and walked up to the cabin on the dirt road. There was enough moonlight that he didn't need to use his headlamp. He was happy for his stealthy protocol upon reaching the cabin and seeing the lights on inside. He'd no doubt guessed correctly that Rob and Sue would be up early, as hikers are known to do. This confirmation of his plan increased his confidence.

After waiting and watching for ten minutes, Volkov committed to his plan by stepping onto the front porch and positioning himself at the door. He wasn't going to storm inside. He was going to wait for them to open it on their exit.

He readied himself with his new hunting knife. The outdoor gear store didn't offer much selection for six-inch blades. He felt length was more important than any of the other nice hunting

158

features of multiple uses. He was interested in the blade that contained a bottle opener on the top edge. This knife's only feature besides length was that it was serrated. That's all he would need. He could shop for that other knife online after he returned home.

***

Sue was standing by the wood-burning stove as Rob prepared to open the cabin door.

"Should we leave this water heating on the stove?"

"I guess not. Pour it in the sink."

Rob was carrying his backpack in his hand in front of his belly as he opened the door. This was fortunate as Volkov charged him, repeatedly stabbing the backpack. Rob stepped backward with each lunge of the knife. Volkov was aware of Sue standing to his side but didn't expect her to be holding a pot of hot water.

It blinded his right eye and seared the skin on his face as she threw it on him. She then whacked him over the back of his head with the empty pot. The stainless steel pot had some heft and dropped him to his knees, wherein Rob kicked him under his chin and laid him onto his back, with his legs awkwardly and painfully folded at his knees underneath himself.

Rob hopped over him and sprinted out the door with Sue into the dark forest.

***

Sara was up early Tuesday morning. The prospect of spending the day hacking into Russian financial accounts to steal their wealth wasn't just the most exciting thing she had ever done, it would likely be the most spectacular thing she would ever do in her life. She found it hard to sleep.

When she heard the sound of her father's coffee grinder at 5:30 am, she took a quick shower, let her hair dry in a ponytail, and picked out her most criminal-looking outfit to wear. She selected a black cotton, mock turtleneck that stopped above her navel, black cargo shorts, and black ankle boots. She made a mental note to take Katie shopping for more ghetto clothing at thrift shops before school started as she joined her father in the kitchen.

"You're up early, pumpkin. Preparing yourself for school to start back up?"

"Morning dad. No, I want to get into work early today. We're doing some pretty cool stuff."

"Anything you can talk about?"

"You know, it probably is sensitive, but no one told me I couldn't discuss it. At least, not since I left the Doughnut."

"I'm all ears, pumpkin." George put down the papers he was studying to listen to his daughter. He knew full well what she was up to because he talked regularly with Calvert. The two had been working together for most of the last decade, with George developing spyware for the Major. Something he absolutely could not talk about.

Sara sat down at the kitchen table with her own cup of coffee with cream.

"Well, I started working with this boy yesterday."

"A boy? You mean your age? Another intern?"

"Well no, he's eighteen. He looks my age though. He acts more like he's fourteen." Sara rolled her eyes. "He's from Macedonia. His name is Josif. He's the little brother of Andrei Popov, the hacker I worked with back at the Doughnut."

"Right. I met Andrei. How'd his brother get involved in all this? He a hacker too?"

"Sort of, yeah. Probably even more of a hacker than Andrei. Our job is to hack into these European financial institutions and transfer funds away from a list of Russian oligarchs. But Josif already had backdoors into every firm. And the only thing that slowed him down breaching all the accounts, was teaching me along the way. He's the smartest hacker I've ever met. And I don't mind telling you dad, with my job this summer, I've met a lot of hackers."

"I suppose you have."

"It doesn't bother you Dad, that I'm doing this?"

George smiled at Sara with a look she understood to be that he knew more then she did.

"I'll let you in on a little secret, Sara. Remember when I prompted you to speak up at BlackHat last summer?"

"I do. You were a bit pushy as I recall."

"That was my way of introducing you to Major Calvert. He was a captain then. Major Calvert and I have known each other, professionally, for several years. I knew he'd be impressed by you. I can tell you right now that if you were interested in attending the Air Force Academy, it's a done deal. He and I talk about you all the time."

"Dadda. Does mom know?"

"She knows about the scholarship opportunity. She doesn't know the extent of the skills you're learning. The illicit nature of some of your jobs. She understands it to be government sponsored and above board. And really Sara, it is. We just can't let her in on how dangerous some of it is." George looked Sara directly in the eyes and said, "Pumpkin, sweetie. You're very special. You've never taken tests but I can assure you, your IQ is genius level."

Sara was too embarrassed at her dad's assessment to respond. She blushed a little. He continued talking.

"We kept you in public schools just to ensure you could relate to normal people. We make up for it with the summer programs, the travel, and all the books.

"And let's not downplay the danger you've been in lately. Don't think I don't know the risks. It's not that I'm not concerned for your safety, but Sara, you're so special, you need to be challenged. You'll be shadowed throughout the school year by CyberCom. Hopefully, not too overtly, but Major Calvert has assured me you'll be provided constant protection given some of your assignments this summer."

George noticed that Sara had been silent for longer than normal. "Am I freaking you out with all this?"

"A little, yeah. Dad, I had no idea you knew about all of this."

"You're a special girl, Sara. Kids with your talents, if we don't keep you challenged, who knows."

Sara knew her dad well. She sensed he didn't want to continue flattering her. He liked to pretend he's tough. Sharing these feelings, this information, was highly unusual for him.

"Dadda. I love you."

"I love you too, pumpkin."

"I gotta go. I want to get in early to start before Josif shows up."

"That's my girl."

***

Rob and Sue fled into the woods as they ran away from Volkov. Rob considered taking their car but didn't know if the General was alone or if the two others from the sushi bar were outside too. He went for terrain he knew he could navigate. Only problem was that he had to power on his headlamp for visibility bushwhacking through the brush.

"Rob, I don't think there are any trails close to the house."

"There aren't."

"How do you know which direction to go?"

"We go up. That's our advantage. We're conditioned for the altitude. We'll climb to the top of this ridge, then take that to where it intersects with the next ridge. There's a trail on that one that will lead us to a twelve thousand foot peak. I forget its name."

"Won't we be exposed up there?"

"I'm hoping we can get a signal on the peak. I can't explain it but I can usually at least text if not make a voice call."

"Okay, but can you slow down a little, please? I'm already winded."

"Then stop talking so much."

***

Sara left her cardigan at home, partly because the conference room was warm with all the computers running, but mostly because it softened up her cool cyberpunk look too much. She was surprised, and a little disappointed, to discover Josif beat her into work.

"You sleep here overnight, Josif?"

"Oh man, there wasn't much sleeping at my place last night. We are attacked by the guys from the sushi bar."

"In your hotel?"

"In the room next door. We have this setup with two apartments. We enter into the first apartment before entering our own. Cybercom lives in that unit. Last night, the Russian mafia guys followed Andrei to our place and broke in."

"What happened? Is Andrei okay?"

"Yes. Cybercom shot the guys dead. The police came. We had to leave and we checked into this place near midnight. That's why I'm already here. Short commute. Andrei almost called your dad. He said we might be moving in with you soon anyway."

"I'd like that." Sara caught herself. "I mean, I'm sure my dad would be fine with that." She hoped Josif's English wouldn't be good enough to catch what she let slip about her feelings for him.

"You're in pretty early too, Sara."

"I was excited to get started."

"Let's go. Andrei explained the game plan to me last night. We're not going to be able to transfer funds quickly enough for our timeline, which is immediate. But we can if we set up new accounts in the same firms as our breached accounts. For example, if oligarch A has his account at Fidelity, we set up another dozen

162

accounts at Fidelity to move his money around in. We never transfer oligarch A's funds outside of Fidelity. The beauty in transferring internally is we'll avoid outside transfer agents. The money will be totally invisible, until we decide to make it visible again."

"Sounds brilliant."

"It is. Sometimes my brother is half smart."

Josif noticed the stitches on Sara's arm as she shifted in her seat.

"Oh wow, Sara, is that what happened from your car wreck?"

Sara knew he'd see it today and had her response ready.

"Yeah. I flew out of my jeep and through a plate glass window at a hundred and fifteen kilometers per hour."

If Josif thought about it, he would have noticed she prepared her response from her expression of the speed in kilometers rather than miles, but his higher faculties were blind when he was looking at her.

"Wow. I've never even driven that fast in a car."

"Yeah. I miss my jeep already. It was all white. Self-parking. Apple CarPlay. It was nothing like these military jeeps we've being driven around in."

Josif was impressed. And in love. He would do all he could to impress Sara in return by teaching her how to illicitly transfer international funds away from Russian oligarchs.

"What do you want me to do, Josif?"

"We'll split this list of banks and trading firms to set up the dummy accounts. A couple dozen per site. I've created credentials for us to use with the notifications on all our actions disabled. I can't stop the metadata generated from the existence of our new accounts, but we'll be done before they notice anything in their logs. By lunch, we should be able to start shifting funds around."

"Brilliant."

***

Volkov was up and on the front porch just after Rob and Sue entered the forest. First, he heard them. Moments later he saw the light from Rob's headlamp. He turned his on too and followed.

Within seconds, he determined he wouldn't be able to run after them. His lungs were already burning. He'd have to walk, maintaining as strong a pace as possible, and hope he could track Rob's light. He wished he had a rifle.

The slope was steep and Volkov was losing confidence with each step. *That American is the luckiest son of a bitch he'd ever encountered. If he could have purchased a nine-inch blade, he would have stabbed him right through his backpack. And that fucking woman. He's going to enjoy catching her.*

As he considered whether or not he should continue, he conceded the odds might well be in Rob's favor. He knew that Rob knew he had the advantage of altitude. That's why Rob was going uphill. Volkov was smart enough to walk at a pace he could handle and play the long game. He might be five or ten years older then Rob, but he was fit too.

He knew he could easily kill him by hand, even without a knife, from their fray in the sushi bar. And he was certain Rob didn't have a cell signal because he didn't himself, and Rob would have run toward the road if his phone worked. The one variable out of his control was other hikers. Should be light traffic considering it wasn't the weekend. Plus it was incredibly early still and it wasn't like they were on a trail.

The General continued his pursuit. He'd play this out, at least until the sun rose.

***

Greg and Andrei joined Sara and Josif in what they called their war room by 8 am. They focused on their DDoS attacks. Greg shared status with the team as he received regular updates from Calvert. By 10 am, Calvert compartmentalized the Internet, which meant he severed connectivity between North and South America and the rest of the world. While Calvert wasn't relaying much intel on the success of Russia's counterattack against America, this told them everything they needed to know. This had never been done before.

They turned on CNN for what Greg termed out-of-band intel. Internet DNS servers were struggling to resolve IP addresses from domain names. Google was allowed to continue answering search queries, but was ordered to disable YouTube as nonessential. Likewise, FaceBook was ordered to shut down. By noon CDT, the equity markets closed for the day. Just as well, the Internet was simply too slow to deliver the expected user experience. Connectivity for the war room was unaffected as they leveraged a satellite connection that proxied them directly into the European Internet, and they used mostly IP addresses rather than URLs.

The team kept working through lunch, having food brought into the war room. By 2 pm, connectivity in Europe was untenable and

164

they had to quit their efforts. Sara and Andrei had completed their mission by then. For extra credit, Sara searched harder for Putin's accounts and believed she might have discovered one with thirty billion dollars in it. She wasn't one hundred percent certain it was Putin but Greg told her to pull the trigger and she emptied the account.

***

Rob and Sue reached a trail after fifty minutes of bushwhacking along the ridge, west of their cabin. Rob had been able to track Volkov's headlamp through the woods and determined they could slow down for a few minutes to stretch and check the water reservoir in his hydration backpack. He knew it had been slashed in the knife attack because the water had been leaking down his back since he put it on. They drank what little remained, knowing they still had a single water bottle. Sue didn't have a chance to grab her backpack during their escape.

"Well that sucks. Still, better my CamelBack than me getting stabbed."

"I would agree, darling. The sun won't be hot for several hours still," said Sue.

"Yeah, I think we'll be fine. There's enough light now on this trail that I'm going to pocket my headlamp. Fancy Bear is going to still need his in the woods. I see him occasionally. He's at least a half mile back."

"You've picked a name for our attacker?"

"No, that's his name. Sort of. The team he leads, or more accurately, the signature they leave behind of their cyberattacks, is termed Fancy Bear. Since he's the leader, might as well call him that. His real name is General Volkov. I forget his first name just now but I know that too. I've studied his profile. He's close to Putin. Real close."

"We're being chased by a Russian General?" Sue was incredulous.

"Yes, we are."

"Good God, Rob. How? Why?"

"Honestly Sue, I have no idea. Maybe I've earned some notoriety from BlackHat last summer. Or maybe they think I work for Calvert. That wouldn't be too far off from the truth at times."

"Has your work always been this dangerous?"

"No. Geez Sue, seriously. Stuff like this didn't start happening to me until I met Calvert last year. I don't need to retire. I just need to unmeet him."

Sue didn't respond. She didn't have to. Her stare was enough.

Rob said, "Let's take advantage of the trail and pick up our pace."

***

Calvert hadn't slept in over 48 hours. The most exciting hours of his military career. No one was calling this Cyber War II. No one was even calling this a war. Russia had labeled the NATO backing of the Ukrainian counterattack against Russian Separatists as aggression. That messaging was being carried by both western media and NATO itself.

Their word choice stemmed from the perspective of conventional war, which appeared to have been avoided. Calvert was delirious knowing this was the greatest cyberwar in the history of the world, even if it only lasted for two weeks. The final day was nothing short of spectacular. Russia proved it could bring America to its digital knees, and for the better half of a day, it did. But Calvert won the war.

Calvert had been called into the war room with the Generals inside the Doughnut to facilitate negotiations with Putin's generals. The objective of Operation Xs & Os was to retake Eastern Ukraine. Given the nearly immediate acquiescence by Putin after Calvert's cyber operations made a quarter trillion dollars in Oligarch money disappear, NATO upped the ante for the return of Crimea. Calvert was directed to a seat at the table. Across from him were seven Russian Generals, on a large video conference screen.

So Calvert wasn't happy to be interrupted by a barrage of text messages from Robert Warner. At least, he thought to himself, he could text under the table. Preferable over leaving the room to take a call from that knucklehead.

***

"Rob, is Calvert there? Is he responding!"

Sue had been in good spirits up until now. Even humorous at times, helping Rob to keep his shit together as they hiked up to the unnamed peak and discovered a sheer thousand-foot cliff on the far side. She began to lose it herself when they saw Fancy Bear emerge from the woods on the trail. The last three-quarters of a mile were above tree line with complete visibility for both them and Fancy Bear.

"Yeah. Got him. He's sending troops in a helicopter. ETA thirty minutes."

Rob obtained a strong enough cell signal on top of the peak to text, as he had hoped.

"Fancy Bear will be here in thirty minutes, Rob."

"I don't know, honey. He's walking maybe a mile an hour. Looks like over a half mile. It took us over thirty minutes to reach the peak from tree line. I timed it."

"We were walking. What if he starts running?"

"His heart and lungs will explode."

"You're suddenly a lot more confident mister."

"Seriously Sue, we're sitting in a pretty strong position here at the top of the hill. I'm just happy he's alone."

"Can we use anything for a weapon?" Sue started to look around.

"Yeah. Rocks." Rob thought back to the previous summer when he found himself in a similar situation. "When he gets close enough, we can throw rocks at him."

At first Sue was skeptical. *Throwing rocks at a man armed with a knife.* Then it occurred to her that they could absolutely throw rocks at him. They could probably kill him. They were sitting on a pile of rocks. She began to collect fist-sized rocks she could easily throw.

***

Volkov was tired and thirsty, but maintained his steady pace upward. He was an experienced mountain hiker. Normally, it was something he enjoyed. He knew the trick wasn't speed, but rather maintaining forward momentum. If his breathing indicated he was exceeding his lactate threshold, he would stop for a half minute. Otherwise, constant forward motion.

As he looked up at Rob and Sue looking down on him, he wondered how scared they were. *They weren't going anywhere. Must be impassable on the other side. He had them cornered. Why didn't he feel more confident? Fatigue?*

The General told himself his plan remained good. He made all the right decisions. Even with daylight, there were no other hikers, probably no one within miles. He trained his thoughts toward who would be better to gut with his knife first. Him or her. If he killed Rob first, he could then take his time with her. He'd like that. *Hopefully they have some water too. Why are they moving apart? Defensive positions? Oh, this will be good.*

Fifty meters shy of the peak, close enough to start shouting at Rob, the General ran out of trail. The remaining path was a pile of scree, broken rocks that further slowed down his progress. He was able to make out what appeared to be possible paths based on a worn out color to the scree. He silently continued his climb, looking up at Rob and Sue as often as his footing allowed.

Halfway up, Rob yelled down at the General.

"That's far enough, General Volkov."

Volkov didn't mind stopping for a brief chat. It would help him catch his breath. These final fifty meters were considerably steeper. He chuckled.

"Mr. Warner. I see you know my name. And your lovely wife, what's her name?"

"You don't have a need to know General. You'll never get any closer than this."

The General wasn't sure where Rob's cockiness was coming from. Probably just bluffing.

"Oh, but I do. Because I'm going to kill you first. Then I'm going to take my time with her."

Volkov wasn't going to allow Rob to stall by playing games. He took another step forward after this last statement.

The scree required him to look down at his footing as he stepped forward. He didn't see Sue throw her rock. She didn't throw it hard as she focused on accuracy, but she had gravity working for her. Accelerating close to ten seconds per meter squared, the rock hit him hard in the chest. Then Rob threw his first rock.

The General cussed loudly in Russian, partly from the pain, partly from the realization that he was in real trouble. The assault was unrelenting. He was able to avoid two out of three rocks but ultimately slipped on the scree and tumbled downward ten meters. The scree piled down on top of him, causing more injury than the propelled rocks.

Bloodied, and with what he suspected were multiple broken ribs, the General understood he would have to retreat as he returned to his feet. He didn't bother looking up at Rob and Sue before turning around to head back down the trail. At the same time, a helicopter came from nowhere and was over him in seconds. Two soldiers repelled down with machine guns. He continued cussing in Russian until they had him on the ground and placed a bag over his head.

Chapter Fourteen

BY Wednesday night, Sara was wearing her second dress in a week. A recent record for her, without counting Sundays when she went to church. The occasion was a dinner date with Josif, to celebrate the completion of their successful role aiding CyberCom to defeat the Russians in what they learned was hybrid warfare.

While evidence suggested the immediate threat to them from Russians invading Austin was over, she still had her military transport, so she rode to dinner with Josif in the back seat of a jeep. She was fine with that. In Austin, jeeps were cool.

Josif and his mother spent the day moving into her parent's house. Andrei and Danica decided they would stay at the Marriott downtown. They were partial to hotels. The plan was for Josif and his mother to live in her house until the end of the month, by which time they would move back to the UK under their newly assumed identities.

Sara and Josif had already worked out an encrypted communication tool they could use to stay in touch, but they wouldn't be apart for very long. Sara's father let her know she'd been accepted into the Cheltenham Ladies College if she was interested. She was. CLC wasn't actually a university in the American sense, rather it was a girls boarding prep school. An internship was also waiting for her at the Doughnut.

Josif held her hand as they walked from the jeep into the restaurant. Sara liked that.

***

Calvert, back home in San Antonio and laying in bed alongside his wife, reminded her that they needed to turn back around for more travel to attend Justin's services in Colorado.

"You know, traveling won't be so easy when you're a mother."

"I'm no one's mother, boy. Not yet. The click-through results on that one haven't been posted yet."

K.C. surprised herself with how harsh those words came out. She changed the topic. She had a story to share with Jamie.

"I'll say one good thing about hospitals, they're a breeding ground for epiphanies and I decided on our baby's name. I had dreams where I could see our little, dark-haired girl. She was a warrior with supernatural power."

"You know it's a girl? You been talking to a doctor?" Calvert asked his wife.

"I don't choose the avatars in my dreams, Jamie. They just present themselves to me."

"Okay. Which power?" Calvert could quote over three dozen and he was always looking to add to his Marvel trivia library.

"A new one. It's subtle. She has one eye blue and the other green. As if to warn you of her pending anger, her blue eye also becomes green. Then she's able to see color emanate from people, like auras. It tells her of people's emotional state before they take actions. She uses it as a fighting technique, to predict her opponents' moves before they strike. And she's lightning fast.

"These were lucid dreams that stayed with me after I woke. Hours later, they were still as vivid as when I dreamt them. I watched her with a bird's eye view. She held position on top a cliff, over the ocean.

"I know. I get the metaphor too. Still, it's what I dreamed. I watched her fight a line of adversaries, strung out over the horizon, like medieval soldiers queued up to take their turn pulling the sword out of the stone.

"Apparently she could take breaks from fighting, because she would talk to me and I could see her blue-green eyes. She was happy chatting with me. Then her face would turn cold and the blue eye would turn to match the green. Next scene would always be her fighting a line of men, one at a time, and beating them based on her power she called colorpthy."

"Colorpthy?"

"That's what she called it. She liked that her eyes were different colors. She seemed sad whenever they turned both green."

"Sounds more like misandry to me."

"This isn't some Marvel trivia competition, Jamie. It's not about some contrived power. She was using her power for good. To protect something. I never found out what. But she was a superhuman guardian of some sort."

"I don't think that's a superpower. I think some people actually can see colors on people. I read about this somewhere. It's a real thing."

"You're thinking of grapheme-color synesthesia. The ability to see colors in words and numbers. Don't think I haven't looked this up. I've literally spent hours online researching this over the last week. Her power is more of what you might call, using the same techno terms, empathism-color synesthesia.

"She was telling me she's a warrior. I branded that into my womb in that fight on the clifftop. And through the epigenetic powers in play at birth, she was born with this ability and melded it into something corporeal that she could yield like a sword."

Calvert read the clues like a seasoned detective and, almost dutifully, shifted into a spoon with his hand on her belly. He let her talk. He liked her bedtime stories. At one point in her story, he spoke to reinforce what he believed was one of K.C.'s messages, that she'd fight to the death to protect her baby's life.

He told her, "Babies are a woman's kryptonite darling."

"Tell me about it. When our baby turns out to be a girl, we're naming her Cyan."

"You got it, darling. I'm so glad to be back home with you."

"We've only been apart for a week, Jamie."

"It was a big week, darling. After the negotiations with those Ruskies, I was told to expect a promotion to Lieutenant Colonel."

"Congratulations soldier. I'm glad you're back too."

***

After the last ice age, Paleo-Indian tribes hunted now-extinct Mammoths and Mastodons on the alpine slopes of northeastern Larimer County. They buried their dead with attentive care, sprinkling them with ground hematite as part of their funeral ritual.

Ten thousand years later, with the same view of the Mummy Range, Meagan held Justin's funeral service outdoors at a venue for such events in Estes Park, Colorado. Food was served afterward in a gazebo standing off to the side of where the services were seated.

Once all the guests left, Meagan planned to stand atop a cliff to release Justin's ashes in the breeze. They were married here.

Rob allowed for most guests to leave before gathering around Meagan with the four other living partners of what was once Response Software. The day before, they completed their transaction selling the firm to Cyber Business International for one hundred and fifty-five million dollars.

"Meagan, maybe this isn't the best time, but hopefully this will help dull the painful memory of today. This check is for Justin's share from selling our firm yesterday. Twenty-five million dollars. We're an LLC, so you'll file taxes at the rate of ordinary income on a Schedule C form."

"Rob, my God, I don't know what to say. I wasn't expecting half this much. Thank you."

"Well, I'm sorry you're not getting this directly from Justin. He was a big part of our success."

"That's very nice of you to say. He loved working with you all."

Rob smiled, remembering some of his time with Justin.

"You know, in my last conversation with Justin, he told me he was going to buy you a house in Montpellier. He was going to move the entire family there to let you train with your team."

"You're not serious? I'd long given up on thoughts of training with my old team in France. I would love that."

"I'll look through his company emails. He was working with a realtor there. I'll forward you their communication if I find it."

"Thank you again, Rob. I hope we stay in touch."

"I'd like that."

The partners all expressed their final condolences. Rob, Sue, Greg and his wife, Calvert and K.C. rejoined in the parking lot, with stunning mountain views in every direction. Rob started the conversation.

"K.C., it's good to see you outside of the hospital."

"Same here, Rob. Sorry I missed your second trip to the hospital the following week. I imagine you've expired your deductible by now."

"I suspect I have," Rob laughed. "Major, I understand you've been promoted. What comes after major?"

"Lieutenant Colonel. It's not official yet. Cyber War II worked out quite well for me though."

"Congratulations."

Rob said this facetiously but Calvert missed it and nodded with a proud smile while Greg had more questions.

He asked, "So, how about a final readout, Major? Did the wind farm breaches have anything to do with the events of the last two weeks?"

Calvert responded, "No, not really. Other than it got me to Europe about five days earlier than planned. And I could tie more casualties to it. Not the least of which was Private Yankee. That Brit was really something the way he stormed that hotel."

Greg agreed, "That hotel lobby was like a scene from a Tarantino movie."

"I imagine it was pretty gruesome. That poor boy wouldn't have been seconded to me if not for the wind farm breach and the subsequent ACH attack. It was really unfortunate."

Everyone nodded and was quiet for a moment reflecting on their midnight exit from the hotel, before Calvert continued.

"I can add this, it's sort of related to both the breach and our cyberwar actions. Sara downloaded transaction history of the Oligarch's equity trades over the summer. A number of them took large positions on energy futures. They made some coin as output faltered in July and August. They were manipulating the markets. And we know that Russia completed their advanced orders for Nord Stream 2. We believe the wind farm campaign was designed to promote either one or both of those activities."

"They lose anything once the breach was detected?" asked Rob.

"Nope. They closed out their positions with impeccable timing," Calvert replied.

"And then you returned all their money to them?" Rob continued.

"We did. Or we will eventually" Calvert grimaced in his reply before adding, "But we got Crimea out of it."

Sue asked, "So that was never part of your original plans?"

"No, totally bonus. The plan was complicated but with the key objective to help Ukraine retake their eastern provinces back from the Russian Separatists. My role was to conduct what we term full-spectrum cyberwar operations as part of our larger defend-forward hybrid war strategy.

"Leveraging Andrei was my primary objective. I probably would have earned my promotion with just that. But then Sara and Josif succeeded in pilfering a quarter of a trillion dollars in oligarch booty. That got us Crimea. Unbelievable. Totally unexpected.

"By the way, Mrs. Warner, really impressive in how you captured Fancy Bear."

"Well, he brought a knife to a rock fight," Sue said dismissively.

Unconvinced, Rob asked, "You honestly trust them to fully exit Crimea?"

"They've already started, and NATO moved their border troops into a few cities. There's a three-month schedule where we'll return their funds while they depart. UN troops will ultimately replace NATO forces. That schedule will be in the news soon but you won't hear mention of the money exchange. Keep that between us."

Rob changed the subject slightly by stating, "I've been reading a lot of negative stories on NATO's aggression, specifically about the dangers of letting our military conduct cyber operations. You call it defend forward, but Russia nearly shut America down last Tuesday."

Calvert nodded affirmatively. "If you only knew how bad it actually was. Man. But you and I both know Mr. Warner, when a cyber storm is brewing, you're gonna want to run to CyberCom for cover."

"Not me, Major." Rob smiled broadly. "As of today, I'm retired from cyber-everything. Sue and I deleted all of our social network accounts."

"You're going Luddite on us?" Calvert asked.

"No, no. I'm still a techie at heart. But I'm reducing my digital footprint. With recent events, I'll be paying more attention to personal security and privacy," Rob responded. "That reminds me, what happened to Fancy Bear? He in Gitmo already?"

"I wish. We do still have him, but he's not talking. And I saw an official request this morning from Russia, demanding his release." Calvert chuckled. "Apparently they just now figured out we have him. He'll likely be exchanged. Edward Snowden would be a fair trade."

Rob wasn't surprised by this. "That's exactly why Sue and I are pulling down the digital shades on our online exposure. We're buying our next house through an LLC to obscure our names in public records. Let me know when you release Fancy Bear."

"Your number is in my favorites list, Mr. Warner."

About the Author

Ed works as a product manager in the tech industry, thinking up new computer security products to launch. He lives in Colorado with his family. He runs marathons. He's hiked the 500 mile Colorado Trail. He drinks coffee like water. If you think you can keep up with Ed, follow his blog, http://arunnersstory.com

Printed in Great Britain
by Amazon

77859352R10107